Tobias Beck

Unbox Your Life!

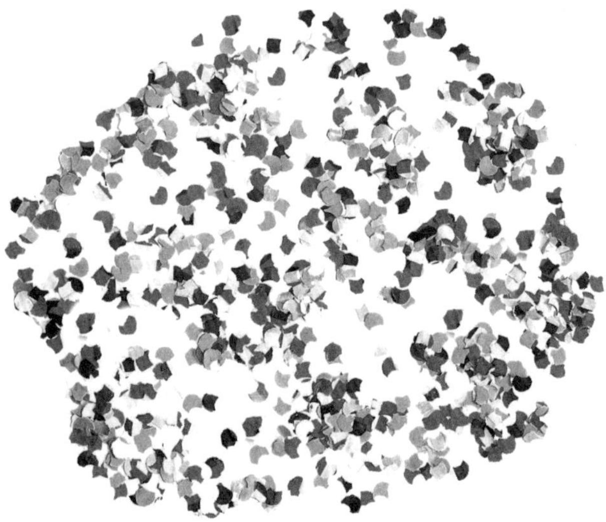

Praise for *Unbox Your Life*

"*Unbox Your Life* will help you do just that—unbox your life and in the process discover your life's mission. Personal discovery and sense of self-worth is the foundation of any healthy relationship which is why the private victory must precede the public victory. This book is a must-read for anyone looking to build relationships that last."

—Sean Covey, President, FranklinCovey Education and *New York Times* bestselling coauthor of *The 4 Disciplines of Execution*

"Tobias shares his struggles and triumphs with raw honesty. This book is a gem. It will help you form amazing relationships, not only with others, but also with yourself."

—John Strelecky, author of *The Why Café* and *The Big Five for Life*

"Tobias Beck is a remarkable coach."

—Daniel Animati, entertainer and TVhHost (*Pro7*)

Unbox Your Life!

Curbing Chronic Complainers, Living Life Liberated, and Other Secrets to Success

Tobias Beck

AMARYLLIS

AMARYLLIS
An imprint of Manjul Publishing House Pvt. Ltd.
• C-16, Sector 3, Noida, Uttar Pradesh 201301, India
Website: www.manjulindia.com
Registered Office:
• 2nd Floor, Usha Preet Complex, 42, Malviya Nagar, Bhopal 462 003 - India
Distribution Centres
Ahmedabad, Bengaluru, Chennai, Hyderabad,
Kochi, Kolkata, Mumbai, Noida, Pune

Unbox Your Life by Tobias Beck

First published in English by Manjul Publishing House Pvt Ltd
By arrangement with GABAL Verlag GmBH

This edition first published in India in 2025

ISBN 978-93-5543-210-0

Printed and bound in India by Repro India Limited

Table of Contents

A Letter from Tobias

From a young age, I had somehow found it hard to fit in. Even in kindergarten, Ms. Zenker had called my mother and instructed her to "pick up [her] son immediately!"

What on earth could such a little boy do to be sent home? Well, I'd been sledding—like all the other students. However, after sliding down the mountain, contrarily to every other child who took their own sled and pulled it up again, I had five girls pull mine back up—with me still sitting in it.

This was the first in a series of expulsions—another one in primary school, and five more in high school—until I was issued an official certificate for learning disability that granted me permission to be stupid. Failure became the story of my life, a story that was told to me so often by others that I began to believe it myself.

The system didn't want me. It chewed me up and spat me out again.

After achieving poor results in my school exit exams, I became a flight attendant and later found myself, via a rather circuitous route, studying psychology. I wanted to find out what was wrong with me. Around the same time—call it coincidence—I ended up with a position in a telemarketing company, which also allowed me to discover some of my strengths. Talking was my thing. The system had never made that clear to me, but I found it out by myself—albeit after more than twenty years.

I became my own guarantor of success, and built up relationships with over a thousand sales partners. Eventually, I became vice president of the company. I had a penthouse with a pool on the roof, a girlfriend who worked as a model, and a custom Mercedes

SLK AMG, which I drove through the streets as if I were the king of Wuppertal.

I really thought I had it all. And I did—until I didn't.

Mistakes were made and, after reaching the pinnacle of success, the empire I'd built collapsed within a week. My monthly salary and sales partners, my savings, my penthouse, my car, and, you guessed it, my girlfriend—everything was gone.

"Was that it?" I asked, sobbing, sitting on the loft bed of my childhood bedroom. Above me hung the David Hasselhoff poster I had taped there as a child.

With newfound modesty, I put myself to work. I slowly got to my feet and embarked on a personal journey to gain happiness and find out what success really means.

I engaged in life-changing conversations with the giants of personality development: Tony Robbins, T. Harv Ekert, Les Brown, and many more. I did my training and put in the hours. I realized that we fight the way we do because we equate success with material goods.

"Moments, not stuff" became my new motto. Changing lives instead of making money became my new mission. Giving back to society instead of taking became my new passion.

From all the adventures, experiences, and conversations I'd had, I derived my personal life principles. As I did so, I found that more and more people approached me and wanted to hear about it. A number of these people encouraged me—or, more accurately, kicked my ass for weeks—until I sat down and finally put *Unbox Your Life* on paper.

In my everyday life, I am a speaker, not a writer. As such, this book is authored in a rather cheeky, unconventional, and entertaining style. It is as far as you can get from literary perfection. Marcel Reich-Ranicki is probably turning in his grave.

Unbox Your Life is bold. I am very much aware of how polarizing it might be. This book is intended to wake you up, scare you a little, and sensitize you. It is based on fifteen years of personal experience in the field of personality development and behavioral psychology. Under no circumstances does it claim to be technically correct.

I have made it my mission to make as many people as happy and successful as possible. For me, chronic complainers, the people from whom we aim to free ourselves, are those who can never be happy and think the world is out to get them, despite having it relatively good. No matter your culture, skin color or creed: do not let the energy vampire in you gain the upper hand. Help those who are truly in need.

For me, this is what "Unboxing Your Life" really means.

Prologue

On the plane to Munich, I glanced at the man sitting next to me and a pair of dead eyes looked back at me.

"The aircraft is always late on this route," he said.

I'd only sat down a minute before, and I'd never seen this man in my life. Yet his words immediately made me want to ring the bell for the stewardess.

You may be wondering why, so let me ask you this: Do you know people for whom *everything* is hard work? People who look for hair in their soup, who are too hot in the summer and too cold in the winter, people who just *know* that the pharmacy leaflet heralds bad news, people who let small details ruin their day, and seem to exist merely to rain on your parade?

Know what I mean? Great. And do you know what I call these chronic complainers? Well, read and learn.

I pressed the button above my seat, and the stewardess appeared. "What's wrong?" she asked me.

"There's an energy vampire sitting next to me," I said.

I registered the shock on her face. "A what, please?"

"An energy vampire," I repeated, without missing a beat. A few minutes later, I was assigned a new seat.

Why did I go to this trouble? Well, because otherwise, my seatmate would have used the entire route from Frankfurt to Munich to tell me about how *hard* life is. That's exactly what "energy vampires" do—and with great enthusiasm! I'm sure you've been in a situation just like mine: when you've wished you could just kick someone out of your personal space, so that positive energy could flow again. I've found out how best to keep these downers at bay—and you're welcome to follow my approach in the future.

Let's go back to the basics for a moment and define what energy vampires actually *are*. Energy vampires are people who Google diseases out of boredom. Energy vampires live according to the lunar calendar and look to the changing of the weather to explain their health complaints. Energy vampires get upset that they cannot rotate the square in Tetris. When energy vampires talk about "goals," they're referring to what they intend to do after work. When they talk about "long-term goals," they mean the weekend—and then they get upset that the day between Saturday and Sunday is missing.

In and of itself, the fact that these people spend their lives in a constant state of dissatisfaction is not a problem. The problem lies in their most annoying habit: they talk! They pipe up to tell such stories as how their third cousin on their mother's side stubbed her little toe on the water butt. And *why* do they do this? Well, it's nothing more than a greedy ploy for attention and recognition. But here's the thing about attention: the more you give it to someone or something, the stronger that person or thing becomes.

I like to illustrate this by imagining the movement of a fan. Imagine that you're fanning air toward a campfire with a piece of cardboard. What's going to happen? That's right—the area you're focusing on will gradually increase in size and strength.

This is exactly how it is with you and the energy vampires in your life. The power of energy vampires grows stronger as they talk to you. What happens next? If you pay too much attention to energy vampires, what becomes of *you*? You guessed it: you become one yourself! Is that what you want for yourself? Certainly not—and that's why I wrote this book. I want us—that is, you and me—to live in a world where fewer people complain about the hole in the doughnut. In the end, most people I meet want only one thing: to be happy by achieving their goals.

I don't have a secret formula for happiness. But for more than fifteen years, I've been working on what makes people really successful. And all these successful people have one thing in common: they live a life without...well, you guessed it: without energy vampires!

***

This book tells of an eventful journey. It tells of my encounters with all kinds of energy vampires, but also with "ants," "diamonds," and "superstars." You'll learn how I found my passion, and how you can find yours. I don't count myself among the most successful people on earth, but I feel internally rich. Every day I live my passion and am able to pass on a piece of it to others, to help them achieve their dreams. If you want to be one of these people, you're in the right place. I wish you an enjoyable read!

Energy Vampires

I use *bewohner*—the German word for "resident"—to describe chronic complainers or energy vampires: people who inhabit a place, but cannot and do not want to positively contribute to the place. They spoil the ambience by bothering their fellow humans with their problems and their constant need for attention and recognition.

Ants

They are satisfied with an "average" life as they do not view things as critically as others. Ants tend to have average relationships. When they find someone, their friends often tell them they could have done better. They are hardworking and cautious.

Diamonds

They are easily recognizable by their glowing faces when they enter a room. They have a positive attitude to life and help you hone your skills. They need the feeling of having taken a step forward each day.

Superstars

They have the highest quality of life and the best chances of success in their work and private lives. If you want to become a Superstar, you have to successfully banish the energy vampires from your life.

I'd Rather Not Engage in This Conversation

I want to start with a story.

"Tobi," Rita said, stroking my hand lovingly, "where we're going tonight, the people are normal. They don't know what you do for work, nor are they looking for a life coaching session. Let's just have a nice evening and go to the balcony if it gets too much for you, alright?"

We were on our way to a birthday party for one of my wife's colleagues, and whenever I'm about to meet new people, Rita sits me down for a briefing on how I am to behave.

If there's one thing you should know about me, it's that I try very hard to abide by the social rules Rita's set for me. On some days, it works wonderfully. But not *that* day. Have you ever been to one of those parties where, despite the spacious living room, the guests choose to crowd the tiny kitchen? This was one of them! As soon as I enthusiastically said, "Good evening," a number of faces stared back in confusion, and I felt the first flickers of irritation. Someone smiled nervously. Someone else gave me a tentative nod of the head. *Oh, not good*, I thought to myself.

"Darling," I whispered in irritation, "is this your colleague's thirtieth birthday, or a funeral dinner for an estranged rich uncle?"

Rita smiled and pushed me in the direction of the prawn cocktail and paper plates.

As I spooned a little of the funeral spread (sorry, I meant the party snacks) onto my plate, I heard someone mumble. "Do you mind being a little careful?" the man said. "I went to the doctor last week and had a ganglion on my foot shaved off. It's still bleeding now. Just didn't want you to step on it."

"By their voice and language, you will recognize them," the ancient philosophers wrote. People who are unsuccessful talk about problems and project them onto other people; successful people talk about ideas and goals.

There he was before me—a man who defined himself through his medical ailments. An energy vampire! The hair on my arms stood up, and my palms started to sweat (yes, in those days, energy vampires still provoked a physical reaction). Since I hadn't reached the bar for an icy drink that could temporarily deactivate my mirror neurons with a brain freeze, I resorted to my ultimate energy-vampire-banishing phrase.

"I'd rather not engage in this conversation," I said, with a friendly smile.

Honestly? A party with prawn cocktail—that I could overlook easily, because of my love for my wife. But engaging with energy vampires in my spare time? No, can't do.

As sympathetic "oohs" and "aahs" began to whiz by on all sides, Rita shot me a pleading look. *Please, don't say anything.* All attention in the kitchen was focused on the partygoer and his foot. And the breath-taking spectacle went even further—because now, everyone wanted to be sicker than the next person, or knew someone else who was. This birthday party soon turned into a pity party. And in the middle of it all, I was trapped, bathed in sweat.

Looking around the kitchen in search of salvation, I found a pen on the fridge and wrote "0800/1110111" on the magnet notepad. If you dial this number in Germany, you'll find a phone counselor on the other end. Laugh all you want, but that's exactly what I did: I referred the bunch of them to a tele-therapist.

I simply refuse to deal with this kind of scenario—particularly in my spare time. I want to maintain my sanity and salvage my precious mirror neurons.

We've now arrived at an important point. Many energy vampires have a keenly practiced hobby, which is that they are only too happy to engage with the topic of illness. Do you know this kind of people—ones who have a backache on Monday, a toothache on Tuesday, a stomachache on Wednesday, and a headache on Thursday? Hopefully, you've already added these splendid specimens on your list of people to avoid. If not, add them now. There are websites, publications, and programs that cater exclusively to this particular brand of energy vampires. There are people who obsess over WebMD, diagnosing themselves afresh with every new ache or twinge. These are the people who can reel off twenty different types of headache if you wake them up at night—and for every type of headache, of course, there is a special remedy. Whole sectors of business make their money off this hysteria.

We must guard ourselves and our mirror neurons like hawks. But be warned: it's no easy task, and even I am not always able to manage it. Recently, I returned from a keynote speech for a big international fashion brand. I was under the weather, so at the Frankfurt airport I hot-footed it to a pharmacy to buy something for my burgeoning cold. After serving me politely, the pharmacist asked, "Do you know that ticks are on the rise?"

"What?" I asked.

"Ticks are on the rise," the lady repeated, in hushed tones. She handed me a small brochure. "Do you have children with you? We're in a pandemic area."

"A *what* area?" I asked myself. As I boarded the suburban train to the city center, my mirror neurons feeling tired and congested, this wonderful publication was in no small part to blame. The airport employee sitting across from me stared in disbelief at the brochure's title page.

I sat on the train and, for the first time in my life, devoted myself to the subject of ticks. A member of the arachnid family, these constantly multiplying creatures lurk perpetually in every shrub and wait for their only chance of continued survival: digging their claws into us and infecting us with meningitis. This happened precisely 234 times in Europe last year. For me, one thing was clear: my careless, unsuspecting attitude had to end, not least to protect my little son. My home state, Hesse, was circled red in the map. Red! That meant *a lot* of ticks. I flicked through the pamphlet in panic. There had to be a solution! On the last page, there it was: for 29.99 euros, one could buy a tick repellent, spray it on the ankles twice a day, and the little critters would stay away.

Exactly seventeen minutes after purchasing the cold medicine in the pharmacy at the airport, I found myself anxiously entering another branch of the chain at the main train station. "One tick spray," I heard myself cough.

"With pleasure," said the clerk—who looked eerily similar to the pharmacist from the airport, another trick of the mirror neurons.

Two hours later, I was home. I lowered the blinds and sat alone at the table, sprayed and stinking (for as we all know, the more of a remedy you use, the more effective it is).

"Tobi, what on earth happened?" my wife asked. "Why would you close the blinds in the middle of the day?"

"We're at war, my darling. 234 Europeans have died in misery," I whispered, in a panicked voice.

Now comes one of the reasons why I love my wife so much. Calmly, she took a calculator and divided 500 million by 234. On this basis, the risk of dying from a tick bite in Europe lies at one in just over two million. I rolled up the blinds and placed the vial of chemicals in the hazardous waste. It's vital to be mindful about the messages you let in. Think carefully about the books you engage with, the news you read, and the TV programs you watch. When it comes to someone like my Aunt Hilda, there's no point asking how she is: all you need to know is in the "bio-weather" report. Toothache is rife in the north, backache in the south, and allergies in the west.

Biowetter = Bioweather, Zahnschmerzen = Toothache, Allergie = Allergies, Bauchschmerzen = Stomachsche, Rückenschmerzen = Back Pain

List five varieties of energy-vampire media that you consume or have consumed:

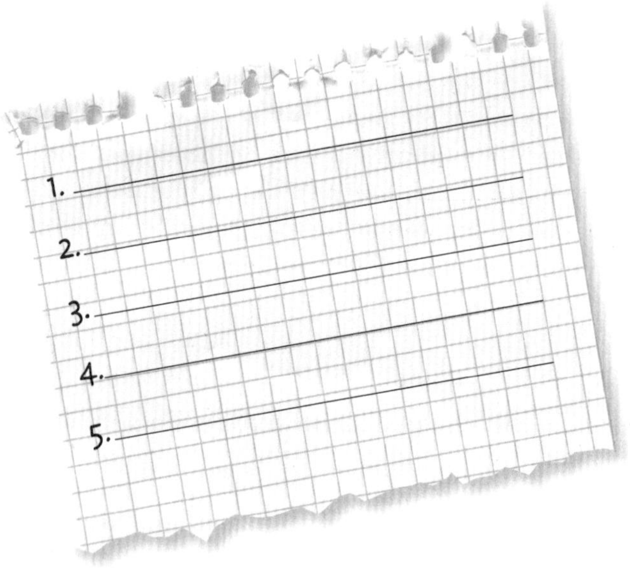

If there's one takeaway from this chapter, it is that you should spend as little time with energy vampires and their panic-inducing media as possible. Incidentally, this negativity also claws away the valuable blue "life particles" you can never get back. If you're wondering exactly what these are, keep reading.

I have rather a personal history with these life particles. Rita and I were in southern India a few years ago and found a magical place, home to a group of people who had made personal growth their life's goal. They helped the local community and distributed books on the street to educate people about personal development. After we talked to them for some time, they took us to a temple with a huge mural. It told the viewer an important story.

When we are first exposed to the light of the world, we are full of little blue globules, the so-called "life particles." Energy vampires feed on these particles. Every time we come into contact with an energy vampire, a small globule moves from us to the vampire and is lost forever. As a child, we have lots of these blue globules and are full of energy and visions for life. But our number of globules is limited, and if we consider how many times we surround ourselves with negatively-minded people, it becomes clear that we need to take great care of ourselves and our resources. What's more, whenever we are negative about ourselves or another person, one of these globules bursts. No wonder some people feel so tired and fed up—their supply of life particles is probably depleted.

How long is the list of energy vampires in your immediate environment? Write down the names of five people who do not add value to your life and are most effective at depleting your life particles:

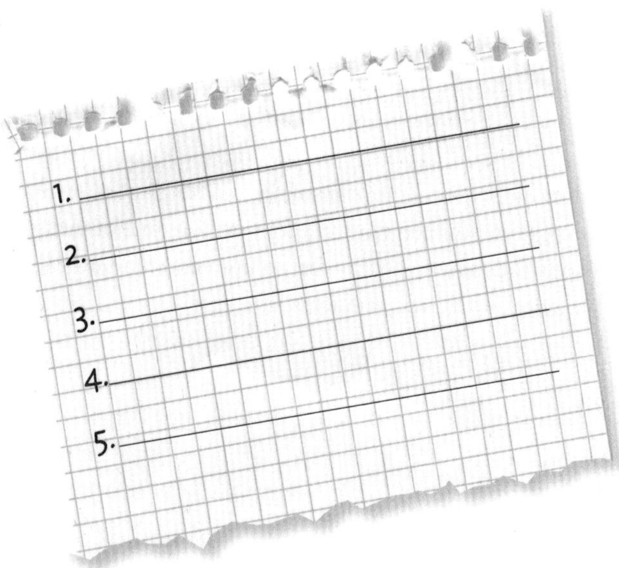

Rita and I were at sea on a cruise ship, where my task was to train the staff and get them ready for the upcoming holiday season. You might assume that being a member of the crew is a relatively easy job. If you did, however, you'd be failing to take into account the guests themselves, who bring their own quirks and do not suddenly become new people by virtue of being on vacation. Do you see where this is going? Yes, energy vampires on board!

After talking for a whole year about this ostensibly wonderful time—finally, a proper reason not to go to the office!—energy vampires begin to complain with gusto about anything and everything on board. They stand on the deck and discuss loudly how proud they are to have claimed nineteen dollars back from the tour operator because the ship departed ten minutes late. The food is always cold, and the fight for chairs is a nightmare. So it goes on.

It was on such a ship that we found ourselves now, and we sought refuge on the furthest deck, where only very few passengers ventured. Out at sea, I observed a seagull, wings motionless, floating effortlessly on the breeze. "What a great photo op," I thought. I fetched my camera, adjusted the lens, and focused it on the bird. Before I could click the shutter, a shrill cry came from the right: "Careful! They're dangerous, these seagulls! If you get bird poo on the lens, you'll never get it off again!"

The seagull and I were startled, and we peered into the eyes of a stout, embittered woman whose face had been visibly weathered by life. Sometimes, when you meet a person, their wrinkles alone make clear that they have zero sense of humor. I was speechless. Following the seagull's lead, I absconded from the scene as quickly as possible to avoid further conversation. I told the staff and Rita the story, and we amused ourselves richly with the amount of effort that some people invest in talking down the most enjoyable time of the year and seeing the negative in everything.

Two days later, as our ship cruised across the Mediterranean, we made ourselves comfortable with a cup of coffee in an area overlooking the pool. Six hundred or more people basked in the blazing sun around an area of water barely larger than a paddling pool. Among them was my new, bird-shy friend. As we people-watched and enjoyed the moment, Rita touched my arm lightly. "What a coincidence that would be!" I followed her gaze and spotted a lone seagull gliding slowly over the ship. "Yes," I answered, "that would be hilarious, for sure!"

We followed the flight of the seagull, and as it flew, its expression changed. Its eyes bulged slightly, its beak opened and its entire body momentarily tensed up. With a soft cry, it relieved itself. A large helping of shimmering, yellow-brown seagull poo shot toward the deck. We watched, stunned, to see what would happen next. *Splash*, it went, and out of all six hundred people around the pool, the bird's excrement landed precisely on the belly of the woman who had ruined my photo session a few days earlier. She jumped into the air and immediately began objecting loudly to the bird, the tour company, and even the sea itself.

What caused this chain of events to transpire? Esoterically-minded readers might cite the Law of Resonance. A worker in a chemistry lab, to whom I told the story later, had a different theory:

mass x seagull x plump woman equals…well, the inevitable.

As far as I was concerned, it was much simpler than that: negative attracts negative.

Make a list of the "diamonds" who help to hone and polish you, or those who have the potential to do so in the future:

1. ______________________________
2. ______________________________
3. ______________________________
4. ______________________________
5. ______________________________

At this juncture, I want to tell you a story. Did you ever have to change schools as a child? Did you ever have to do it more than once? I certainly did—and that included two different kindergartens! The result was that, at the age of fourteen, my mirror neurons and I ended up at a comprehensive school, where I'd later go on to meet my first ever "superstar."

I stood in front of my class on the first day. "Hello," I said matter-of-factly, "I'm Tobi, and I have a certified learning disability." I held up my certificate as evidence (laminated, by that point, because I needed it more and more frequently). If my school career thus far had taught me anything, it was to make light of your weaknesses and wear them on your sleeve. The certificate was like my personal trademark.

This school was where everything would change. A single statement shifted the course of my whole life. The teacher slowly and deliberately opened a drawer, took out a big pair of red-handled scissors, took the certificate from my hand, and cut it in half. I remember her exact words: "Tobias, if you accept this label, this label will become your story. What becomes your story becomes your life, what becomes your life becomes your identity, and what becomes your identity becomes you. Starting from today, we're going to learn math differently."

From that moment on, my mirror neurons and I learned math in a way suited to right-brain, creatively-minded learners. Much to the relief of my parents, I even passed my high school exit exams.

Why am I am telling you this story? Well, I want to show you that there *are* people who change the lives of others. They don't necessarily do so consciously, but rather by simply living their own passion. There are people for whom work is not work, because they do exactly what they love; they give something back with their whole being and their whole heart. For me personally, that's what makes me a successful person. Success is not what's in your bank account; it's not having a job where you feel important and can hide behind an impressive title, either your own or your parents'. Success, in my world, is what comes from you. Success is when you are passionate for a cause and make yourself deaf to the negativity in your environment. Success is when you enjoy every breath of life;

when you wake up with the realization that you have the potential to play a part in the stories of many others. Most wonderfully of all, you can be successful by doing exactly what you love. On the following pages, I'll tell you how to pursue this path.

Take the Personality Test

Before we go any further, I want to give you a little freebie. Do you want to have more influence on other people? Would you like it if people would do what you tell them to do? Every human being is special in his or her own way! However, there are certain characteristics which indicate how a person acts in his everyday life, his career, and his or her relationships. We've designed a ten-to-fifteen-minute test that lets you determine your personality type. Check it out!

Answer the following fifty questions.

Question 1: If there is a problem, I ask myself how this problem arose.

True! False!

Question 2: I am a self-confident person.

True! False!

Question 3: I love to analyze things and work on them until I understand every detail.

True! False!

Question 4: Working on my own projects is easier than working in a group.

True! False!

Question 5: Others readily allow me to lead them and people trust me.

True! False!

Question 6: People do not need authoritarian structures in order to work efficiently.

True! False!

Question 7: I am the right person when it comes to giving instructions.

True! False!

Question 8: Competition is not important—only the work itself is.

True! False!

Question 9: Reading newspapers and watching the news are part of my daily routine.

True! False!

Question 10: I love to analyze philosophical issues.

True! False!

Question 11: Experiencing adventures and discovering new things make me feel good.

True! False!

Question 12: What others say about me is very important.

True! False!

Question 13: I know exactly who are the people in my life whom I can trust.

True! False!

Question 14: My fellow human beings respect me.

True! False!

Question 15: Material security is more important than being successful.

True! False!

Question 16: Having expertise in a field is more important than being socially competent.

True! False!

Question 17: I am an overly cautious person.

True! False!

Question 18: My expertise affords me many advantages.

True! False!

Question 19: Sometimes I am too tough and cold-hearted.

True! False!

Question 20: It is important for me to do my job well. I am not responsible for innovative thinking.

True! False!

Question 21: It is difficult for me to accept hierarchical structures.

True! False!

Question 22: I love speedy procedures.

True! False!

Question 23: Discipline and decency are important values.

True! False!

Question 24: The company I work for needs to exude a warm and cordial atmosphere.

True! False!

Question 25: Other people value my expertise.

True! | False!

Question 26: It is difficult for me to take risks and stay strong, even when necessary.

True! | False!

Question 27: It takes a long time for me to trust a person.

True! | False!

Question 28: I am not satisfied until every detail of my task is completed.

True! | False!

Question 29: I enjoy collecting things and putting them into order.

True! | False!

Question 30: Life consists of giving and taking.

True! | False!

Question 31: I am what some might call a control freak.

True! | False!

Question 32: I would never judge anyone, but what I do not tolerate is giving up.

True! False!

Question 33: I am a rather reserved person.

True! False!

Question 34: Creative thinking is one of my strengths, and I am good at adapting to new situations.

True! False!

Question 35: It is easy for me to work in a team, but I would never lose sight of good competition.

True! False!

Question 36: I am the mediator in groups.

True! False!

Question 37: I am not good at losing and I often insist on my rights.

True! False!

Question 38: When I am successful, I want the world to know it.

True! False!

Question 39: I don't have much endurance and quickly give up.

True! False!

Question 40: I have the ability to motivate my colleagues and to drive them on.

True! False!

Question 41: As long as I love my job, it is not important how much money I make.

True! False!

Question 42: I find it important that the company I work for is successful.

True! False!

Question 43: Being successful is the most important thing in life. Everything else is secondary.

True! False!

Question 44: I sometimes tend to avoid problematic situations rather than solving them.

True! False!

Question 45: My head is full of innovative ideas.

True! False!

Question 46: Whenever there is a problem, I immediately have a solution.

True! False!

Question 47: I am a traditional person. Old-fashioned values are important.

True! False!

Question 48: I am a determined person, whom no one can easily bring off-track.

True! False!

Question 49: It is important to me to have a secure and fixed position in a company.

True! False!

Question 50: The person with the most energy always wins.

True! False!

Evaluation of the Personality Test

The questions that you have answered can be used to identify four different kinds of person, which differ greatly from one another with regard to their overall orientation, view of the world, attitude to work, and their own identities. All of these types are of equal weighting, and they are indispensable for companies and society in general.

Very few people can be categorized as belonging to a specific type. In most cases, several types are combined. However, this sort of classification is a useful method for characterizing people.

Many companies use personality tests to find out which area a new employee would be best suited to, taking their skills into consideration.

Check the box if you answered "True!" for the corresponding question. Now, to find out which animal type you are, count the number of checkmarks in each column. The higher the number, the more prevalent this personality type.

	Owl	Dolphin	Whale	Shark	Animal Wonder (Equal parts: Owl/ Dolphin/Whale/Shark)
1					○
2		○			
3	○				
4					○
5				○	
6		○			
7				○	

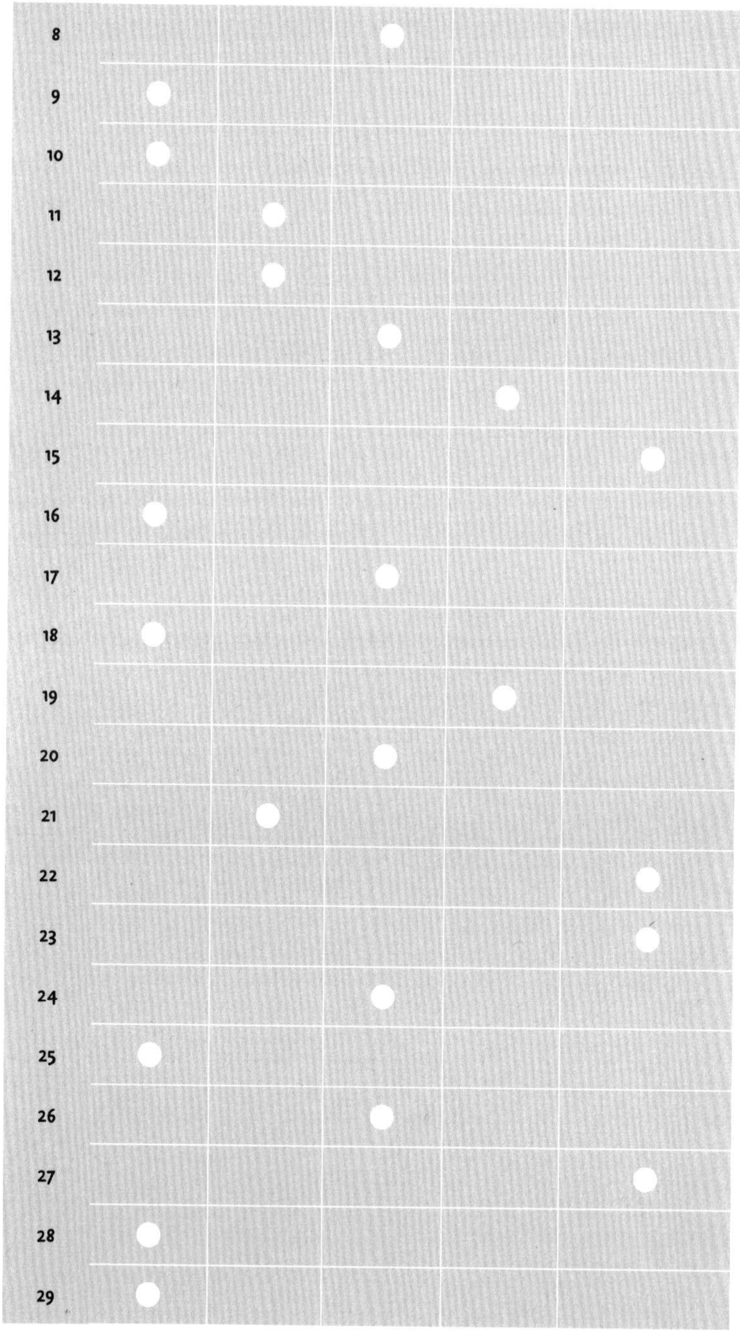
8
9
10
11
12
13
14
15
16
17
18
19
20
21
22
23
24
25
26
27
28
29

30					●
31	●				
32				●	
33			●		
34		●			
35				●	
36			●		
37				●	
38				●	
39					●
40		●			
41		●			
42			●		
43				●	
44					●
45		●			
46					●
47	●				
48				●	
49			●		
50		●			
TOTAL					

Four types have been established:

Owls

Owls focus on the work itself, and not so much on the money, fame or career possibilities. Owls like everything to run according to plan; they also like to develop, collect, and organize things. Quality and perfection are just as important as specialized knowledge, skills, and discipline. When looking for a solution to a problem, they work in a well-thought-out manner and don't like taking risks. When working with others, they ensure the focus is put on resolving the actual task in question, and they are always well informed and well prepared.

Owls are generally quiet, sincere, modest, and practical. However, they often struggle with their own standards as to quality, which can be excessive. They very rarely watch TV, and when they do, they are very selective as to what they watch. They would rather occupy themselves with activities that improve their performance, and like to challenge themselves. They love everything to do with technology and computers, and often spend their free time tinkering with things or completing further education courses. Knowledge, technical know-how, skills, hard work, ingenuity, discipline, and respect for others and their accomplishments are the principal elements of an Owl's identity. Owls like to get to the bottom of things and discuss them pragmatically. However, they are often taken advantage of by Sharks and Dolphins, who steal their ideas and use them for their own benefit.

Owls rarely want to be the head of a team or group, because this would mean they would have to supervise Dolphins and Sharks. When working in a team, challenges are often created by their perfectionism. If this occurs, Owls will often complete most of the work themselves instead of delegating. They are always afraid that something could go wrong. If errors do occur, excessive criticism is often the result. Owls often also react aggressively toward themselves, if they are responsible for making a mistake.

Owls love technology, and are very cost-conscious, correct, professional, and generally somewhat conservative. When communicating with an Owl, it is important not to lose the thread and to always have an answer to any question. Owls often find it difficult to keep the technical side within limits and be generally understandable when communicating. They can work well with Sharks and Whales; they do not, however, get on very well with Dolphins.

Dolphins

Dolphins love challenges and having fun, and view life as one big, fascinating adventure. They enjoy competition, sport, and activities that allow them to prove themselves. They always sit in the front row, and are very communicative and unconventional. They like taking risks and encouraging others to make more of an effort than usual. They treat work and life as a game. Competition gives them a real boost, they can pass on their enthusiasm to others, and they are generally bursting with energy.

They like new ideas, new techniques, fresh, innovative methods, and shortcuts. They talk and think in a simple, clear, dynamic, and playful manner, but are sometimes a bit impulsive. Dolphins like taking calculated risks and always see possibilities. They are cooperative, would like to be superstars, and often fight against bureaucratic structures. They do not focus their energy on obtaining wealth, since honor and pleasure are more important to them; they also like to be seen as winners. Dolphins are not afraid of competition. To the contrary: actually, they feel challenged, inspired, and invigorated when competing with and measuring themselves against others.

They enjoy having their fingers in many pies at the same time, and find it difficult to concentrate on just one thing. Equipped with a considerable portion of sensitivity, intuition, and possibly also a certain amount of positive craftiness, Dolphins can always ensure that the right people come together. They do this in an offhand yet elegant manner, and always manage to encourage people to work for them. They instinctively avoid people who are destructive and negative.

When a Dolphin is the leader, meeting rooms resemble crew cabins where objectives are discussed in a humorous and spirited manner. Sharks and Owls have difficulty getting used to such an approach. Dolphins focus on pulling instead of pushing and try to enthuse colleagues and customers about themselves and the products, instead of discussing things in an unemotional and factual manner.

Dolphins tend to be liberal and enjoy risks; they also like to rebel. They are high-spirited, hardworking, enthusiastic, and open to new ideas. However, they sometimes have difficulty recognizing their own limits, and are often more dependent on others than they would like to admit. They want to maintain the illusion of limitless options; this can limit their capacity for social responsibility, however. Dolphins like speed, become enthusiastic very quickly, and are willing to invest a lot of money in those things that provide them with pleasure.

Dolphins can work well together with Sharks and Whales. However, they find it difficult to deal with Owls.

Whales

For Whales, it is very important to feel wanted and be a member of a strong, protective group that provides them with support. They are willing to sacrifice themselves for others, are tireless workers and always worried about whether they are still needed or not. They generally deal with the human side of a company, and are usually inconspicuous and quiet. Their interest in the needs of others forms a basic part of their character, as does their ability to generate a pleasant atmosphere with their balanced and caring ways. Whales value a good atmosphere, security, and cooperation. The word that best describes them is "integrator." Whales tend to become completely absorbed in their activities, and therefore often forget themselves. They arrive early, remain until late, and often take over work from colleagues.

In doing so, they ensure that everything is kept in order, and chaos and hectic activity tend to scare them. Whales are very modest, responsible, loyal, and caring. Family and friends are very important to them, and they often keep pets and stand up for animal rights.

They always know who belongs to which team and how far they can go without crossing the line. Competition doesn't really interest them, as they don't like to be the center of attention. They are viewed as trustworthy, but not particularly exciting. When Whales are alone, they often feel lonely and lost.

They lack the ability to take risks, are not very tough, have little self-control, and are not energetic enough to draw attention to themselves. They often ask themselves whether they can trust Sharks and Dolphins, who are always very sure of themselves.

If Whales are not careful, they can easily be taken advantage of by others.

When dealing with Whales, it is important to be empathetic and to speak calmly; praise and recognition are also very important to them. They seldom make decisions on their own, and often need encouragement and a lot of support.

Sharks

The objective of a Shark is to obtain power and status in society.

They always put themselves first, and do everything they can to avoid losing control. They view life and work as a kind of jungle, where the motto is "Eat or be eaten."

Sharks tend to forget others once they have set their minds to something. They need to be successful, and don't believe that anybody will voluntarily help them to achieve this. They never change their point of view, and always push their projects through, regardless of the consequences. They are extremely hardworking and focused, thereby motivating peak performance. Sharks are extroverts, are tough, and like to play with fire. They are capable leaders—alpha leaders, you could say. They do, however, cast off unnecessary ballast quickly and are not good at dealing with the emotional outbursts of others.

They love sports that allow them to distinguish themselves, always flaunt what they have achieved, and gloat whenever the opportunity arises. Sharks are proud of the fact that they are feared, and justify this by stating that fear encourages people to work harder. They generally view teamwork as arduous, because they hold the view that they are more successful when working alone. Another strength of Sharks is their ability to look to the future with a great deal of self-confidence and forget the past quickly. They are always willing to take on new projects and are often utilized in situations where drastic measures need to be taken.

Sharks are used to receiving good service, and are often short-tempered if their expectations are not met. Efficiency has the highest priority. They find it very difficult to deal with Whales, as they cannot generally come to terms with the Whale character. Servility is foreign to a Shark's nature. They are also confronted with challenges when managing Owls, since the Shark generally tends to focus on the target instead of taking time to deal with the individual steps. Sharks can have a lot of fun with Dolphins and value their company.

Sharks are quick decision-makers and don't generally waste time with the small print when the value of a product or service has been explained in a manner that corresponds to their way of thinking.

Animal Wonder

If you get this result, you're a rare and wonderful mix of the four previous types! Celebrate that you have multiple strengths, but be on the lookout for your weaknesses too!

What Gets You Out of Bed in the Morning? Find Your Passion!

"The time is right to make a change." You've probably noticed that the willingness to do this is precisely what sets diamonds apart: they take every opportunity to sharpen their skills and make improvements to their lives. Are you ready to leave Energy-Vampire-Town, and if so, how best can you and your mirror neurons make it happen? To answer this question, look again at the superstars in your life and consider what they can teach you about living your passion. Are you already doing this? To find out, take a critical look at your current situation.

Write a spontaneous list of one to five words or phrases to describe your daily working life.

1. ____________________
2. ____________________
3. ____________________
4. ____________________
5. ____________________

Finished? Okay. If you've written things like "Planet of the Apes" / "money generator" / "mental asylum" / "pit of wolves" or "just okay," then work is the first area in which you need to make a change. According to Germany's WSI Collective Agreement Archive for wage tariffs, we spend an average of 1,650 hours at work every year. This adds up to 16,500 hours over ten years and 49,500 hours over thirty years (2017 figures)! According to the World Economic Forum, Americans work 1,780 hours per year on average.[1]

Do you really want to sacrifice decades of your life to "just okay"? Would it not be much more gratifying to say that you are able to give something back in your job and have fun? Can you imagine the long-term effect it has if the only pleasure you derive from your working life is to spin on the office chair? Exactly—you'll end up completely dissatisfied. Once this sets in, you'll start telling your energy-vampire colleagues that the world is a terrible place. At some point, your only pleasure will be to switch on the TV in the evening and dull your pain with alcohol. That can't be all there is, can it?

---

1 www.weforum.org/agenda/2019/03/where-people-work-longest-and-shortest-hours

With this in mind, my first piece of urgent advice is to *think about what you really enjoy*. Is there a path you would have taken in a parallel universe? Is there a dream you've always secretly had, but never trusted yourself to say out loud? It's time! Talk about it—just not with an energy vampire! All they'll do is Google statistics and horror scenarios to scare you away. You see, energy vampires don't want you to change. Energy vampires want everything to stay the same. They want to keep their audience. This brings me to my second piece of advice, which is to *delete all the energy vampires from your list of contacts*. It might seem brutal, but this is a vital act of self-preservation for you and your mirror neurons. As the German saying goes, "Those who follow the herd just end up staring at others' butts." Instead of doing this, surround yourself with people who'll work with you to realize your vision and perhaps even make it better.

List up to five people with whom you share a common vision:

1. ________________
2. ________________
3. ________________
4. ________________
5. ________________

If I had to picture you now, I'd say you're sitting, pen in hand, scratching your head and pondering hard about what wishes and dreams you carry inside you. If you wonder why it's so hard for you to engage with this topic, let me offer a reassuring explanation: you've simply forgotten how to do so. There is a phase of life in which dreams, hopes, and faith come easily to us: our childhood. As children, we are full of visions. The world is an adventure—a playground of possibilities just waiting for us to take hold of them.

Burdensome energy vampires like your old Uncle Keith, who told you that you'd never be smart enough or good enough to achieve your dreams, were easy for you to refute, to hit on the head with a metaphorical spade. Unfortunately, not long afterwards, your education intervened. At the age of six, you ended up at school, a place I often refer to as the "dream destruction machine." Our education system teaches children one thing: to sit down and shut up. Sadly, this dates back to a time in which its main purpose was to produce obedient workers or loyal soldiers. It was important for pupils to conform to a system, which is why many schools still offer rigid curricula instead of adapting to children's individual needs. Often, schools are lifeless, cold buildings with a hallway in the middle and classrooms splitting off to the left and right, just like army barracks. They are generally not good places for unimpeded development.

What's more, although virtually everything save for our school system has evolved over time, we still wonder why, after so many years of schooling, there is a generation sitting in front of us that has no idea what they want to do. When a young person leaves school, they should be equipped to know how to stand out from the crowd. Unfortunately, during their school careers, they learn exactly the opposite: to adapt and conform as effectively as possible. How many of us were taught how to sell, lead people, inspire others, or start a business? That's right, none of us—and that's why it's all the more important for us to relearn how to dream!

It's because of this that I'm inviting you on a wonderful journey, a journey to your inner self. Find out what really satisfies you and what will make you happy and ultimately successful.

Are you ready?

To begin with, I'll ask you to write a few things down.

What inspired you as a child, outside of school, and whom did you find particularly inspiring?

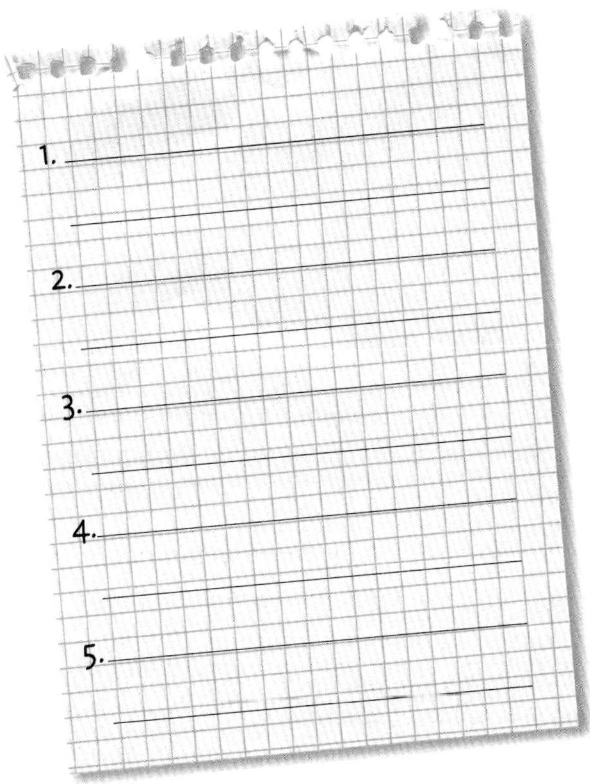

How I Found My Passion

I could tell you that success and happiness came into my life easily, but this would be a lie. On the contrary! As you already know, my school career was anything but sparkling. When I finally graduated from high school and my parents dared to hope that their son would find a sensible occupation, I was as confused as many others by the question of how to spend the rest of my life.

I was clueless—or rather, there *was* an option available to me, but it involved everything I did not want for myself. Yes, it involved four weeks of vacation a year, but the rest of the time, I'd be slogging away, and I would barely be able to afford the mortgage payments for a small condo. This was not a real option. In a similar vein, I was unwilling to squander my life for the dreams and visions of others. That would have been my personal nightmare.

My path led me first to Brazil, where I taught English to street kids and got to know a completely different way of life. It was a life marked by warmth, the celebration of simple things, living in the here and now, and appreciating small blessings like a chilled can of Coca-Cola—something that was not widely available day-to-day in a place without electricity or running water. My Brazilian host family lived alongside me in their tree house and were grateful for every small thing they had.

Many people are unable to do precisely this—to show gratitude for the small things. Most of us only live for days off and vacations. Unfortunately, when this happy time rolls around, they usually spend it getting upset: someone has removed their towel from the lounge chair, it's too warm, it's too cold, it's too wet—or whatever else. I still remember my time in Brazil with a great sense of gratitude, because the people there taught me about a simpler life.

What happens in Brazil...

After Brazil, I came back to "real life" in the Federal Republic of Rules and Regulations. Immediately upon my arrival at the airport, I was reminded of the beliefs that had been drummed into me during my thirteen years of schooling. You'll likely have encountered the kind of people who strive laboriously to have everyone understand how important they are—people who are so busy with their smartphone that they don't have time to get a ticket from the machine. They're the people who shout, "Let me through, I have somewhere to be!" from the back of the airport check-in line; people who blow themselves up like pufferfish, talk only about themselves, and never stop showing off. Does anyone come to mind?

Create a list of five major "pufferfish" in your day-to-day environment. These people are on the wrong path, and you need to be aware of them.

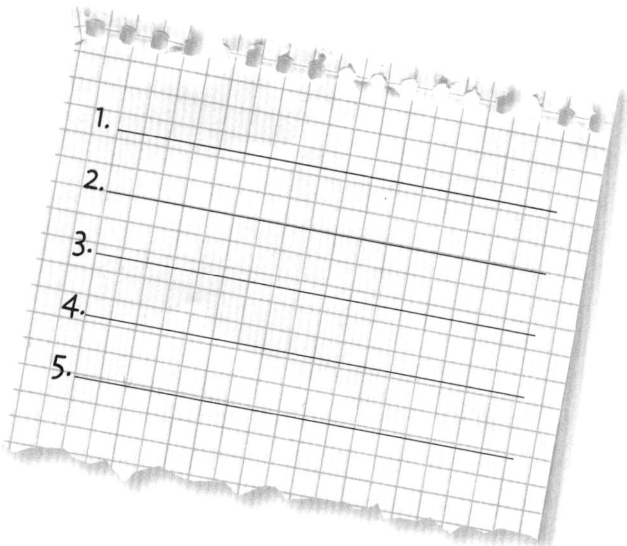

It was this kind of people with whom I found myself sharing the elevator as soon as I arrived in Frankfurt. I greeted them with a friendly smile and a "Good morning," a custom I'd picked up in Brazil. No reaction. Eventually, one of my soulless companions looked me in the eye and said, "It's Monday, kid. You'll get to know about Mondays too." There are times when a single sentence has a lasting impact on the rest of your life, and for me, this was one of them. As this stranger spoke, I knew it in my bones: I would never become one of those people for whom every experience comes via a Wi-Fi signal. No chance! After my return, I deliberately searched for life pursuits that would allow me to give something back—and I succeeded, first with the fire department, and later as a flight attendant.

I learned what it means to work as part of a team and to rely on others when things are (literally) going up in flames. I learned to put myself and my needs second and to serve others, and learning to serve "pufferfish"—albeit with gritted teeth—was, in retrospect, one of the most important lessons of my life.

I honed my knowledge of human nature on my travels around the world. As a flight attendant, I had the chance to talk to some very successful people in first class. I quickly realized that if someone was able to spend fifteen thousand euros on a flight, they were a person from whom I could learn something. Once more, the difference between those who worked to survive and those who lived their passion was obvious to me. I started taking notes during flights and got to know many great and successful people, including Pope John Paul II, pop idol Michael Jackson, German statesman Hans Dietrich Genscher, and more.

The long flights offered the opportunity for a chat, and I often waited hours for the right moment to ask my question: "How did you get to the place you're in today?" Though the answers were often banal, they were nevertheless extremely valuable. Michael Jackson simply told me that he loved music, while Genscher—a well-known politician—smiled and replied that he wanted the best for his country and had learned to always take a step back. In first class, I noticed how many passengers used the time to read, and I took down the titles of their books.

Business class was full of people who slept through the entire flight—utterly exhausted by their work, they were pale and irritable. By contrast, in first class, people spent their time reading and listening to audiobooks. On one of our trips to Brazil, I brought a passenger a glass of champagne, and we chatted for a while. He offered me a piece of advice. "Tobi," he told me, "everything you take in with your eyes and ears comes back out of your mouth at some point in the future!"

From that moment on, I read everything I could about motivation and personal development. Why? Well, I had imagined that I only needed to adopt the behaviors described in these books in order to achieve similar results in the future. After some time, however, I came to a dead end: I wasn't progressing any further.

From the outside, I was the epitome of success. Not only did I travel and study a lot, I'd set up a sales business, and it was going swimmingly. Financially, I was thriving. I drove an expensive car, lived in a luxury apartment with a pool, held fancy parties, and my girlfriend worked as a model.

But none of that made me happy.

I was trapped between the world I knew from the books and the reality I was actually living. With each day, my dissatisfaction grew. My smile became a professional mask. My motivation was like my liquor cabinet on the morning after one of my parties: depleted. At some point, it became impossible to go on; I couldn't stand my job or the people around me.

By 2000, I was, without a doubt, the most practiced "energy-vampire attendant" of the entire airline, which is why, when I received a letter from the company in late 2001, I saw it as a sign. In an attempt to reduce its staff numbers, the airline was offering severance pay. Finally, there it was: my chance to be truly happy and find real success! I signed up immediately for the severance pay and started planning for a new trajectory. I had read about a company that offered its own Happiness University, and my hopes crystallized around that vision. Surely, satisfaction would be waiting there for me!

To my great joy, my application to a subsidiary of the happiness-focused company was successful and I got a summer job abroad. To be able to attend the Happiness University, employees had to prove their worth for at least one year. The company was one of the world's largest "dream factories" and operated several amusement parks where grown-up men and women ran around in various character costumes. When I arrived, I learned of a "probationary period" that lasted a few weeks, during which I was to be randomly assigned to play one of the characters. I remember my lottery number to this day. As a colleague looked at my ticket, 4432, he shook his head sympathetically and said, in broken English, "That's no good." I could have been a prince or a flying elf. Instead, I became a duck—more precisely, I became part of a duck trio, whose identity you've probably already guessed. Unfortunately, the lottery had not taken into account the size of the actors, which meant I waddled as a six-foot-three-inch duck between my two five-foot-tall Japanese "brothers."

My costume weighed a whopping forty pounds, I was squeezed into skin-tight leggings, and I dragged with me the two containers that would provide me water over eight hours of work. My daily commute by boat was two and a half miles, which didn't help the situation: two and half miles in incredible heat under a heavy duck's head. My inner energy vampire had already decided that this job wasn't going to make me happy. When I reached work in the morning, I was already worn out. And the workload was difficult: we dealt with eighteen to twenty-five thousand visitors every day.

What question do you think the children asked most? Yes, you've guessed it: "Why is one so big and the others so small?" After a while, I felt so silly that I snarled at our guests and made fast movements to scare the kids away. I was patently in the "My life is so difficult" and the "Me, me, me" phase. Only much later did I realize that these thoughts were taking me down a one-way street: an untenable and unsustainable path.

After fourteen days, I had had enough. I committed the worst sin possible for someone in my role: I took off my duck's head. I didn't want to do it anymore. I didn't care about anything—even the two hundred or so howling children who believed my character was real. I was an energy-vampire duck, and I thought only of myself. "I just want another job," I complained to my fuming supervisor. After a flood of verbal abuse, the wording of which I would rather not transcribe here, he looked at me sharply and said, in a dangerously calm voice, "Of course. You'll get a better job. No problem."

Well, that had worked fantastically! At last, I was free. Elated, I climbed into the car that was to take me to my next post: a shadowing role with one of the company's drill instructors. I was driven to a different part of town, where my driver allowed no more than twenty seconds for me to climb out of the car and make my way to the front of the house.

I knocked on the door. Suddenly, Anthony, my future mentor, stood in front of me. He was a six-foot-six African American man with impossibly broad shoulders. "Shit! You're white!" were the first words out of his mouth. After that, he bundled me into the back of his van and drove me around the streets. During our short tour, he yelled to all the neighbors that I was his new mentee and that anyone who took me for a fool would be playing with fire. Welcome to my new neighborhood! I was completely dumbfounded. Everything was different here than in Wuppertal.

At dinner, I tried to persuade my mentor to tell me what awaited me. He leaned across the table. "Tomorrow, German Boy, you're going to get to know my life." As it turned out, a day in Anthony's life began at five in the morning—in a yellow school bus! The energy vampire in me couldn't believe it. Had these stupid people still not understood? I wanted to learn to be happy. How could a bus driver help me? We had buses back in Wuppertal. Flummoxed, I allowed Anthony to seat me at the back. I crossed my arms and slumped in my seat as we drove off.

As my inner energy vampire wallowed in self-pity, I was distracted by the shouting of children. "Tony, Tony, Tony!" A horde of students stormed the bus enthusiastically and greeted Anthony with nothing short of euphoria. Each and every one hugged him warmly or planted a kiss on his cheek. I watched the action unfold, my mouth open. Now this was different from Wuppertal! Before me was a pack of joyful, excited children—and at each stop, it grew in size. At one of the last stops, I experienced an even bigger surprise, one that was to have a lasting impact on my life. Waiting for the bus was a girl of six or seven. Even today I can see her clearly, red bows in her hair, a yellow backpack on her shoulders. Anthony opened the bus door, stood up, and played "Happy Birthday" on a small guitar. The whole bus joined in. After that, Anthony reached under his seat and pulled out the "magic box": a lovingly decorated shoebox, covered with aluminum foil, and filled with toys and sweets from which the birthday girl was to pick a treat.

A real superstar: my friend Anthony

I sat with Anthony during the break. "So, when did you take a guitar course?"

He looked at me questioningly. "What do you mean?"

"Well, you must have been sent on a course," I said. "Or perhaps you did all this just because you wanted to?" It was my attempt at a joke—I can still see Anthony shaking his head. "I didn't know you knew so little about life, German Boy."

At the end of the day, we sat together at supper. I was completely lost in my thoughts. Never had I felt so bad and so exposed.

"You're not a bus driver," I said.

"No," Anthony replied. "I just love kids. And if you live your passion, too, you'll never have to work a single day of your life."

I sat there in a heap of misery. Anthony was a great person. He was happy and made others happy; he gave something back to the world. What about me? I pitied myself and cried my heart out to his wife. I was like a little child—but I had realized something important: Happiness doesn't depend on what you have or what you earn, but on what you give to others. When you start living by this rule, your life will become amazing. Anthony was my personal superstar, and he changed my life like no one else.

I had the privilege of living with Anthony and his family for a few weeks, and during that time, I learned a lot about life. In the evenings, we often lit up the grill together and ate corn on the cob with butter and salt. We sat on his little terrace and talked about his values and happiness. Gratitude was an important topic for him, and one which he repeatedly addressed. It reminded me of my host family in Brazil—and it was time for me to be grateful too.

One thing that Anthony did was to give me a blank piece of paper on which to formulate my thoughts.

1. What are your values?
2. What do you believe in?
3. What are you grateful for?
4. Who is your family, aside from your blood family?

This time in Florida was one of the most formative of my life, because I lived with a superstar who would never refer to himself as such.

Over the course of my life, I've also run into other superstars. In 2015, Stuttgart hosted the National Achievers Congress, and I was given the golden opportunity of moderating the event. At that time, I wasn't working for a fee—I had yet to prove my worth to "Success Resources," the largest seminar company in the world, and one with whom I now have an ongoing contract. I stood weak-kneed behind the stage and watched the hall fill with thousands of participants.

Gradually, the first speakers filed in. Some of them paid me no attention, not even to say hello. What causes people to develop these airs and graces, especially in our industry, where we are supposed to serve? This is something I've always wondered. Worse still, I found that all the speakers became extra-friendly the moment they realized I was the moderator. Such people are lost to me instantly. I'm more interested in how someone treats a person when they don't expect anything in return.

Too big an ego can be the ruin of everything a person has built. Often, energy vampires have the biggest egos—they talk only about themselves, and the universe is expected to align with them. But things don't really work like that.

I had chance to experience that firsthand that evening, when the door at the back of the hall opened and a shining star of our industry entered the room. Les Brown—a speaker who had addressed more than 100,000 people over his career—was standing in front of us. My mouth fell open. For years, he had been one of my greatest role models. I could recite all of his YouTube videos backwards and had absorbed his books and CDs like a sponge.

He came up to me, shook my hand, and asked how I was. "I'm well, Mr. Brown," I stammered.

"Tell me, my friend," he asked, "why are you so nervous?" I explained that he was a great role model of mine and that it was a huge honor for me to get to know him in person. After that, something magical happened. Les invited me into his dressing room and asked how he could help. He had reached an age where his sole motivation and interest lay in giving back to others. In the dressing room, he spent two hours answering my questions and coaching me. It was like a movie—one that unfortunately ended far too fast.

A real role model: Les Brown

Before he went on stage, Les spent ten minutes standing with his wife. They held each other and prayed, humble and grateful, that so many people had attended the event. At that moment, another speaker came off the stage and declared arrogantly that he had just sold the German audience more than 200,000 euros' worth of follow-up seminars. Les looked up for a moment, shaking his head. Once more, I realized the difference between give and take. Les and I are still in contact today, and I remain deeply impressed by him and his way of dealing with people. He makes others a star and doesn't take himself seriously. He is a true superstar.

Write down the names of five people who have made a positive difference to your life—your list of personal superstars:

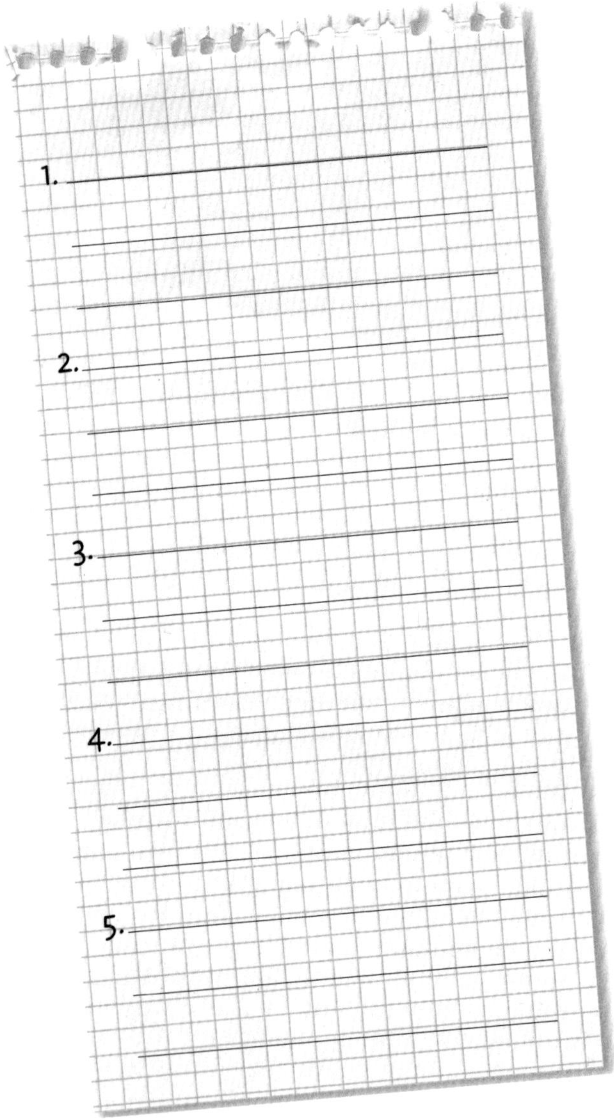

Mentors and Superstars

Conversations with Ruth

The slip of paper exited the printer of the Wuppertal fire department. "Dialysis trip," it said. Now eighteen years old, I sat in the ambulance in my fire brigade uniform and observed the world outside the bubble I'd grown up in.

On my first day, after just six weeks of training and a brief hospital internship, I was well and truly thrown in at the deep end. Far from being a passive observer, I'd assisted a home birth in a stairwell, two resuscitations, and an accident on the highway. A dialysis trip should be a relatively easy one, I thought.

The first time I saw Ruth, I had to smile. There was something about her. A small, neatly dressed old lady with a red hat, she sat on the edge of her bed in the nursing home. "Glad you're here, young man," she said to me. "Everyone else is here to die; I'm here to live. Let's take a trip."

"Hm." I coughed slightly and consulted the information on my notes. "We'll take you to the clinic for the dialysis now, Miss..."

"Ruth. Call me Ruth!"

"Okay, Ruth. Let's go."

"Great," Ruth said, "we're going to the dialysis machine. How fantastic that such a thing even exists!"

She touched up her lipstick, linked her arm firmly through mine, and walked with me down the long corridor, beaming with pride. We passed the rooms of her fellow residents, elderly people who spent most of their day staring into space. Ruth was wholly impressive in her manner and made a nice change from our usual patients. During the twenty-minute drive to the hospital, we sat in the back and talked—or rather, she entertained *me* and told me about her life. She'd lost her husband and two sons during the war, been severely injured by shrapnel, and had struggled to make ends meet. After forty years working in the city archives, she'd been given a golden ballpoint pen and simply dismissed.

A great experience serving others

Even as Ruth told of her experiences, she smiled from ear to ear. She was different from the others. During our trip, she spoke with utmost positivity about her life: about the nurses and other caregivers, the good food in the home, and the miracles of medicine that could now cleanse her blood. Fridays meant semolina pudding, and she looked forward to that for the whole week. In the months that followed, I drove Ruth to the clinic several times, and we became good friends. I told her about my family and brought her nut chocolate, which she was always quick to hide in her purse.

At the time we became acquainted, Ruth was eighty-nine years old. According to the doctor's diagnosis, she was dying: she had been prescribed bed rest, and we were to carry her around. But she did not stay in bed, and she certainly did not want to be carried. She planted flowers in the small garden in front of the home, and whenever the weather allowed, she sat on her balcony and enjoyed the sun. She was always dignified and mindful of her appearance.

When I'm old, I want to be like Ruth. Because of her good nature, Ruth was an exception—one of a kind among the energy vampires who complained relentlessly in the nursing home. She was happy about everything, and her secret was gratitude; she was infinitely thankful for everything she had. She showed me things I had long been unable to see for myself. In fact, one week before her death—an event that affected me greatly—she took my hand and spoke to me earnestly.

"Tobi," she said, "I don't know how long God will allow me to stay here. I trust that on the other side, I'll be able to see all the people who have meant so much to me on my journey. I've been able to feel true love, have children, and live in a country that cares for me in my old age. Your journey is still ahead of you, and I want to give you a gift." Her words moved me. "My gift to you," she continued, "is this very moment. For in the end, that is all we have."

At the time, I didn't understand what she meant. I was still very young, and it was only years later—when I realized all at once how transient life is—that it all became clear.

All we have is the present moment, the here and now.

Since I came to this realization, I've been doing my best to gather moments instead of material goods. I try to anchor meaningful images and ideas in my heart, because when I'm old, I want to be like Ruth. I remind myself to take pleasure in the way and enjoy the journey—because the journey is unique, and every moment so infinitely valuable.

Ruth also gave me a letter.

My dear friend,

After all these years, you have no doubt grown old. Do you remember the dreams you had when you were young, when you talked bright-eyed about your future? Have you achieved everything you wanted? Have you kept that childlike spirit, the one that allows you to embark upon each day with an overwhelming sense of joy? I hope so.

I am rich because I've always done what I wanted to do. Most people spend their whole lives dreaming of their dreams. Those who permit their thoughts and desires to become reality are those before whom the whole world bows. They are warriors of light, and statues of bronze are erected in their honor. It's not the critics, doubters, and complainers who receive the glory, but those who are ready to enter the fight.

I hope you achieve this in spite of the "great fear"; the one that lies dormant like a virus in every human and takes possession of so many. It's the fear of living our dreams, of freeing ourselves from the scourge of others telling us how to live. It's the fear of not being enough, not being loved, not meeting our own standards. This fear is why most people play the game of life small, preferably without risk, and without real contentment. Real contentment can only be achieved by playing your own game. You are a son of the universe, a daughter of the sun and the moon. Your brothers and sisters are the trees, the rivers, and everything that lives. You are no use to anyone if you play small, if you hide your light under a bushel. Burn brightly—because then you can ignite others.

Are you changing the world, my friend? Are you doing what you're supposed to do? Anyone can make little changes to be happy. Some compose music that appeals to the heart and stirs up emotion. Some teach with angelic patience, even though they only see small successes. Do you love what you do so much that you wake up in the morning without an alarm clock and cannot wait for the next day? There are people who cry on the day they are forced to retire. They love what they do. Let me ask you something: if your time were up tomorrow, would you be happy with what you have achieved? If money ceased to matter, would you still continue? I hope so, because the journey is much more important than reaching the destination.

Do you feel that you're often faced with stumbling blocks? Do you feel that times are hard? Let me tell you something: times have always been hard. But let me tell you something else: the time when others are faltering and complaining is your chance to have strength. It's in times like these that others need your strength to recharge their batteries. And if you falter, too, just remember: if you got up this morning and were healthier than you were sick, if you have clothes on your back, food in the fridge, and a roof over your head, you're better off than 85 percent of your brothers and sisters on Planet Earth. Are you healthy? Then you're better off than all those who won't live to see tomorrow. Hold your head up and stop complaining, my friend. From today, you shape your future.

You have respect for the future, and your goals are so great that they may scare you. I hope so, because you need something unattainable before you; something that drives you and will continue to do so. And remember: in the moments of our lives when we cease to ask who we should be, but simply are, our lives shine like stars in the sky. Beware, though, since at some point, you'll realize that even the sun's rays burn when you get too much of then. Then, you'll need people who are able to catch you.

Starting today, I wish for your life to become a fantastic journey. Enjoy it, my friend, because it is unique, and you'll never get a chance to live it again.

All my love,
Ruth

Now, look at the "measuring tape" of your life. Where are you located? How much time do you think you have left?

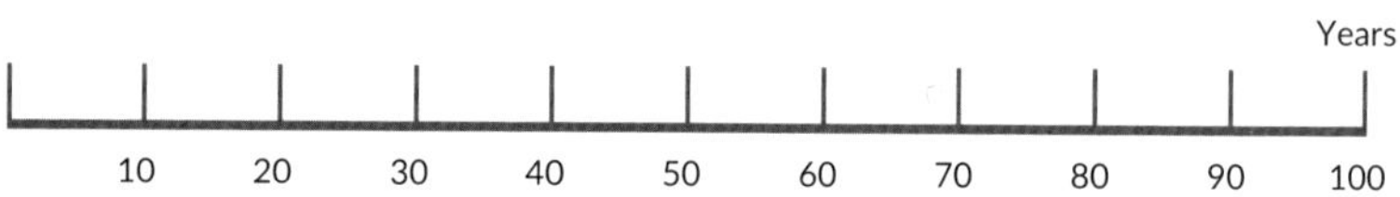

What Now? On Mentors and Superstars

You may have heard the saying that a teacher only enters the life of a student when the student is ready. Life mentors and superstars seek out the people in whom they are prepared to invest their time and energy. They deliberately look for diamonds who are already shining, those who only need a little polish. You must have invested a lot in yourself and your development before you're able to access the inner circle. With my own mentors, I recognized a pattern: they consistently put me to the test, plunged me readily into cold water, and asked me the right questions. If you're looking for a mentor, you should have good answers for the following; otherwise, you'll quickly fall through the net. Read the list below, take a few notes, and reflect on whether you're ready to be polished:

What books have you read in the last month?

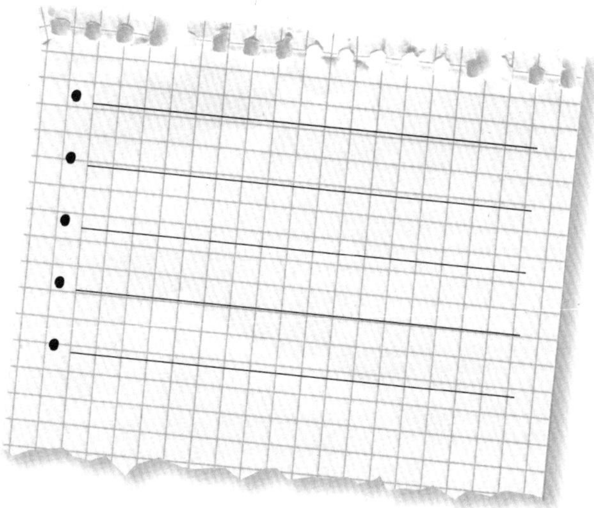

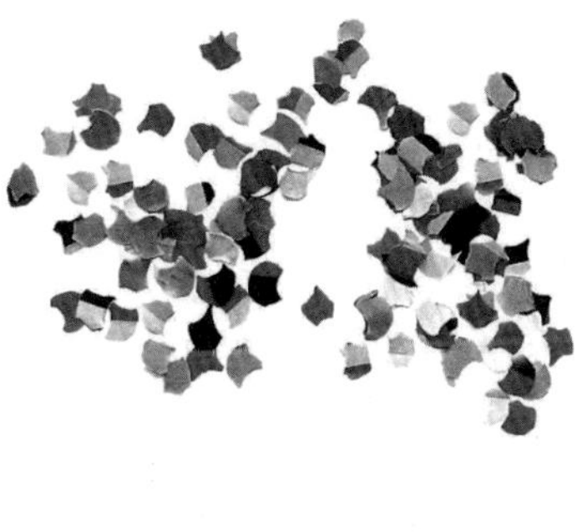

What did you do for other people last month?

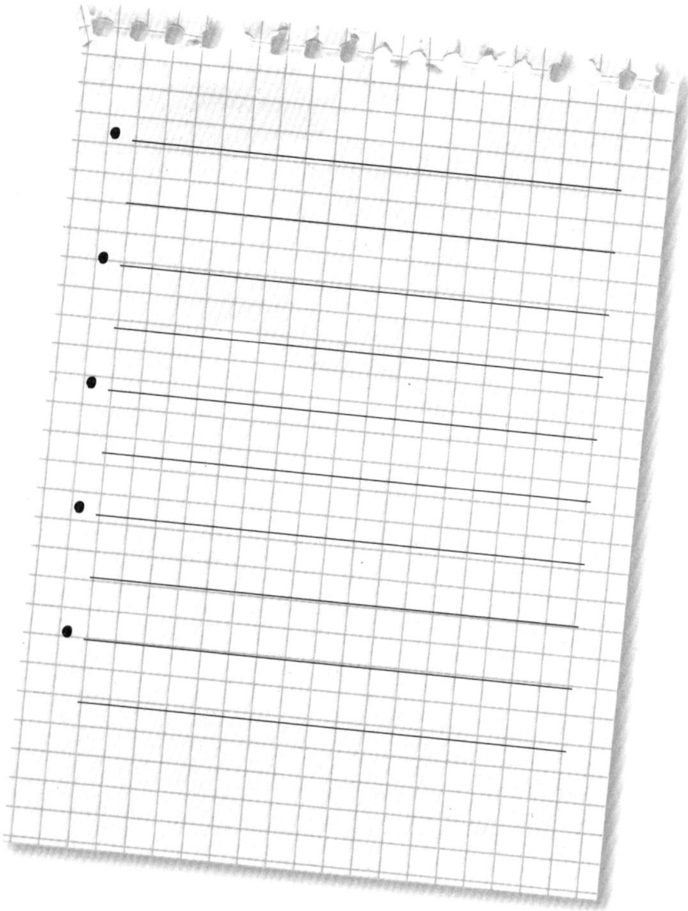

Why are you doing what you are doing?

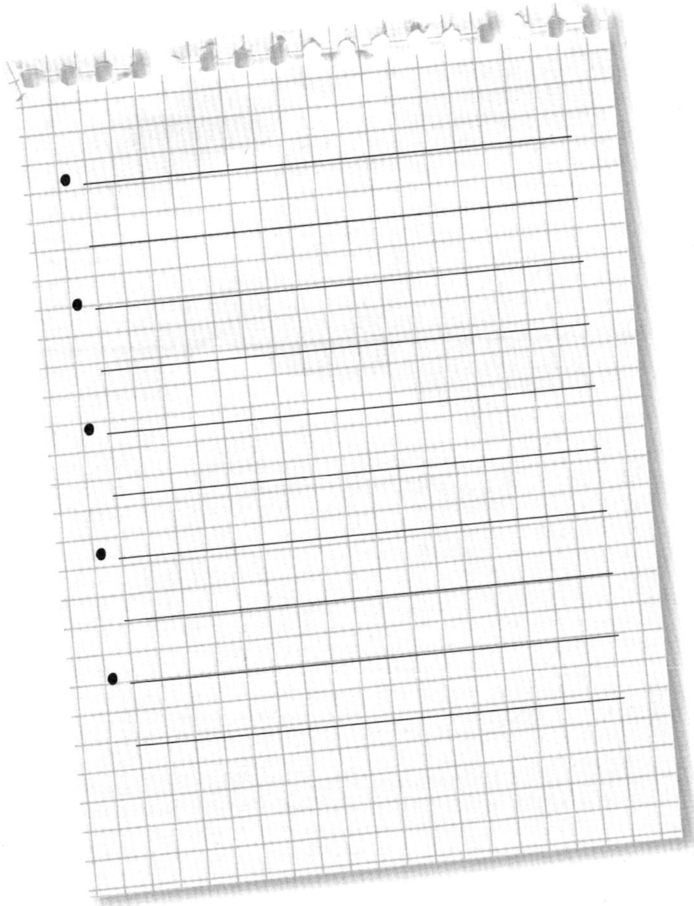

Which seminars did you attend this year to further your education?

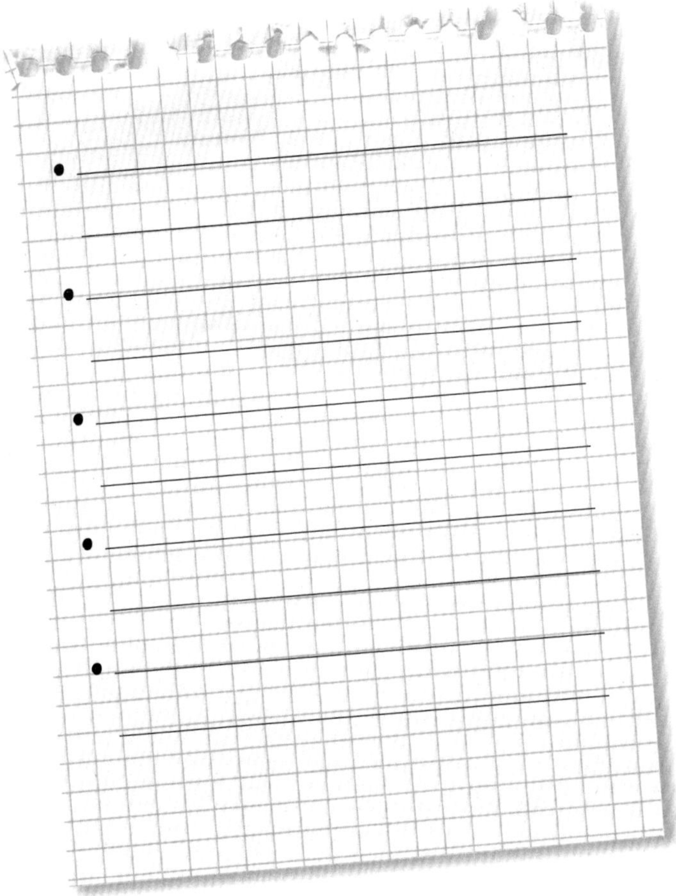

How do you engage in society?

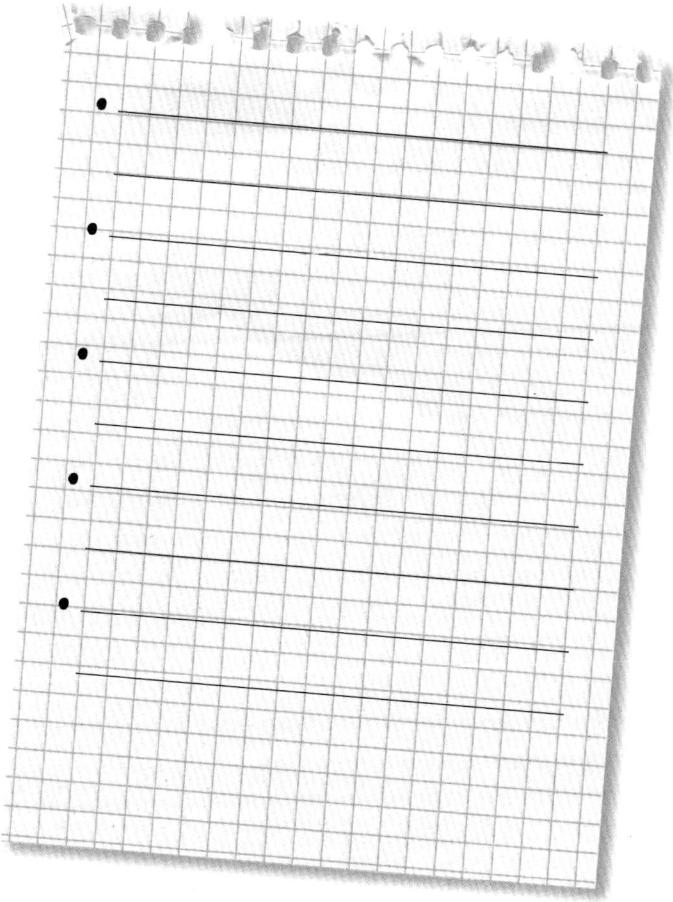

Lastly, don't forget that even mentors are human; they themselves make mistakes. Like you, they have only twenty-four hours in a day—and as a result, they're very picky about how they spend it. When you deal with a mentor, be aware of your energy and your mode of expression. Instead of asking what they can do for you, turn the tables. What can you do for them? Pay into the relationship account before you start withdrawing. Even as a young man, I served as a mentor for some; young speakers, in particular, often look for effective tips and coaching to succeed on stage. What strikes me again and again is that most are simply not willing to pay the price of success. That's why I put any conversational partner through an intensive test before deciding to invest time and energy into the relationship.

But there are also very clever candidates, those who skillfully maneuver themselves into the field of vision of those they want to learn from. Some time ago, I received a handwritten letter in which the sender bluntly laid out the reality of my miserable posture and untoned muscles. The letter ended as follows: "From now on, I'll be your personal trainer. I'll coordinate with your schedule and come to your home whenever you feel like it. I'd also be happy to train your wife. Best regards!" What do you think happened? Jens, who approached me personally in this direct manner, now comes to us twice a week and has virtually become part of the family. During our training sessions, I tell him the secrets of the great speakers and how it's possible to become financially free. It's a relationship of give and take. Of course, Jens had already listened to all my CDs and was well prepared and, above all, hungry. Personally, I always look for the fire in people's eyes. When I see the flame blazing, I'm happy to help. When I see flickering tea lights, unfortunately, I'm out!

What Are You Waiting For? Change Your Life

The million-dollar question: how many times in your life have you made the decision to change something? To lose weight, to say no, to tell a colleague your opinion, to stop smoking, to look for another job. Next question: how many of these things have you actually achieved? If you're currently mumbling a vague answer and feeling the urge to skip this section, do not fret! Humans are all the same. We all have goals; we all strive for change—but the implementation can often go awry. Are you aware of the two key drivers that can really help you effect change? If not, let me introduce pain and desire. No change can function without at least one of these sensations—and you're welcome to test this theory for yourself.

Let's begin with pain. When are most people really prompted to lose weight? The motivation comes, for example, when the individual concerned has severe physical symptoms and is left with no choice but to finally drop the extra pounds. Alternatively, a person might bump into their one-time crush at a ten-year reunion and, instead of falling enthusiastically at their feet, think only, "Wow, you've gained weight!" This is often sufficient as a motivation to take action. As far as smoking is concerned, there is one measure—admittedly very drastic—that rarely fails to take effect. Smokers under hypnosis are mentally connected to a heart-lung machine and required to say goodbye to their family—for best results, to small children. Incidentally, any desire of mine to smoke and take drugs was lost during my time in the ambulance service, where my various conversations en route to the lung clinic left a serious and lasting impression.

Now, let's turn to the second factor: the desire to do something. Are you one of those who find it impossibly difficult to learn a foreign language? Take my Uncle Rainer, who fell in love with a Chinese lady at the age of sixty-four but had the problem that his dear lady spoke neither German nor English. The desire was greater than the pain, and within a short time, Rainer was speaking quite decent Chinese.

The concept can be extended to other areas of life. How often do you really issue an unconditional "no" in the workplace? If pain is solely what drives you, this will probably only occur at the point when your desk is heaving at the point of collapse. But when the factor of desire comes into play—for example, if you're eagerly anticipating a concert in the evening—a staunch "no" becomes the medium of choice in the face of additional tasks. In a similar vein, when's the last time you really told a colleague your opinion, when your level of ire became so intense that you couldn't hold back any longer? When's the last time you and a colleague found a fresh understanding after a company outing, and you sought out a quiet moment to tell them the things that were bothering you? My advice is simply to be honest and stop sugar-coating the issues.

Some time ago, I had a client who was completely burnt-out from his work. When I asked if there was anything positive about it at all, he replied, "Sometimes, when someone's having a birthday, there's cake and sparkling wine." Well, then—cheers!

Pain and desire influence our decisions. They move us to make a difference, to change things. At points in my journey, I, too, have resisted taking action for change until I was hit by the painful realization that I am not living my passion.

My work as a coach has allowed me to gain plentiful experience of the things that instill desire and pain—and one story stands out especially in my memory.

Some time ago, I received a call from the managing director of a parts manufacturer in the automotive industry. "Are you this motivational mogul I've been hearing about?"

I confirmed, laughing, and inquired what he was looking for.

"Well, none of our drones came to the Christmas party this year, and I wondered if you'd be able to do anything about it," he said.

Drones? Had he really just referred to his employees as "drones"?

"Well, I'd say your employees probably hate you," I concluded, appealing for a chance to talk at his company.

My first encounter with these "drones" stays with me to this day. We met in a room filled with beer tables and a small stage. The room was chock-full of the same image: people who were still standing, but were mentally and emotionally dead. I embarked cheerfully on my talk on motivation and gratitude and reaped a mixture of empty looks and ignorance. Suddenly, one of the employees jumped to his feet. "So, you really have it all?" he yelled. "I'm putting a stop to this, you asshole. Take your motivational shit home." The room was revived, and there was a standing ovation from his colleagues. Just as the *Titanic* had crashed into an iceberg in 1912, so I was standing in front of a similar obstacle now. I tried not to go under.

All right, Beck, new plan! I asked for a short break and telephoned the manager. "There's a little problem with this group," I whispered into the phone. "No, to be honest, there's a big problem."

"So—you too!" the boss replied. "Last week, we had someone come to do some in-company education. All the employees had to make a duck and race it in a paddling pool!" At that moment, I realized something. In-company education? No wonder the group wasn't responsive anymore. "I have an idea," I said to the manager.

As I explained my brainwave, I was forced to insist—for the second time that day—that I was still in possession of my senses. Instead of twenty-five ducks, I ordered twenty-five sports cars for the employees to play with. The rest of the day was spent breathing life back into my participants at 130 miles per hour on the highway. These people needed to feel the value of what they were doing, that they and their work were needed. At the end of the day, we sat together in a much-improved mood and reflected on our time together. A couple of them even offered the occasional smile—a rather unusual sight during working hours.

I asked the heckler from the morning's talk to sum up his job in one sentence. He grinned. "I'm racing a car, you asshole!" Everyone laughed—but this time, I laughed along. Incidentally, the company today has brightly painted walls, a saltwater aquarium, and its own brass band, which passes through the rooms every Friday to create a good atmosphere. What's more, the employees volunteer in a nearby kindergarten and give back to society. Since my time at the company, the managing director has recorded a significant increase in productivity and has revised his management style by attending a number of training courses. He's been particularly grateful for a falling sickness rate: when people enjoy going to work, they don't fall ill with every bug going.

So, what have we learned from this story? Yes, that nothing changes without pain or desire. These people were not aware that their important work made them part of a much bigger end product. Only through the driving experience did they gain access to this realization. When you're thinking about changing something, your next question should always be, "What's my reason?" Where is the incentive for you to really live your change? Is it *really* possible for you to progress further at work, or are you standing still?

To illustrate this clearly, I want to tell you a little story. Are you familiar with the definitions of thermometer and thermostat? A thermometer measures the temperature; the thermostat is responsible for regulating temperature and keeping it at a certain level. As humans, we mentally record the temperature from morning until night, and since our brains are geared to protecting ourselves from danger, we're drawn to wherever our "comfort" temperature prevails. But in the shelter of a cave, growth is rather difficult—which is why we need people to adjust our thermostat for us.

I was in Singapore for a refresher course when I met a US coach over a coffee break. We got along great, exchanged ideas, and, at some point, began to talk about our industry. Rather boldly, I asked him what he earns (incidentally, unlike in Germany, this is not a problem for Americans, because talking about money is completely normal in the United States). He mentioned a number—$25,000—and I impressed upon him that it was a good monthly turnover. He looked at me with some frustration and said, "Not per month, my friend, per day."

I struggled to keep my composure. "How can that be possible?" I wondered. Here was someone who made more money in one day than I did in my previous life as a flight attendant in a year. At that moment, I experienced a fascinating thought. I asked myself, "Why not? If he can, I can too." My thermostat was, figuratively speaking, newly reset, and I decided to invest more in my personal development. I would need to venture further into too-hot or too-cold areas to get closer to my goal. But more on that later.

Write down the thermostats—the goals—of your life:

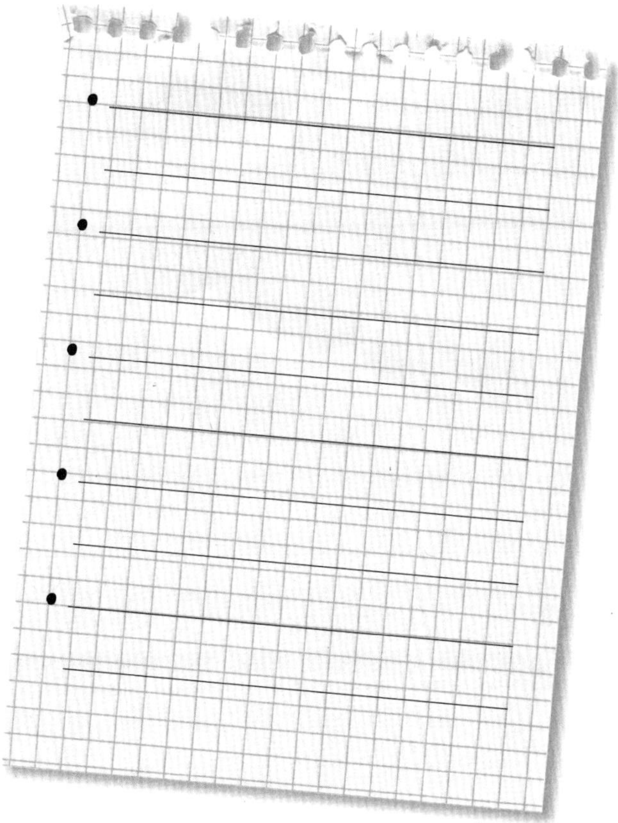

Giving Back: The Four Categories and Happiness

Over the course of this book, I have repeatedly stressed how important it is to give something back. Perhaps you have already thought about what you give back to others—and why this is sometimes so difficult. On this last point, I have something valuable to say. (Note that the following model comes originally from one of my great role models, Anthony Robbins.)

For each of us, there are four areas of life that have an impact on our emotional world. Have you experienced those moments when everything is great? When you love your family, even your mother-in-law? When everything is going well at work, and you feel secure and strong? When you feel centered, you're in the "flow," and everything is just so? In these moments, you feel you could embrace the whole world. These are the moments in which we are able to give back the most. In order to achieve this optimal state, all of the four key areas of our lives need to be in perfect balance. We'll now go through each one in turn.

Adventure

As you know, adventure begins where routine ends. It doesn't matter whether you're an energy vampire or a superstar—everyone loves adventures, big or small.

The difference is that everyone defines adventure according to their individual experiences. For the energy vampire, a visit to the football stadium is an absolute adventure in itself. For weeks, they dream about the away game, ironing their jersey and practicing the team chants—and in the end, the only thing they have to feel happy about is drinking too-warm beer with their mates. Mind you, that doesn't stop them from drinking five or six in the first half alone!

If an ant wants to experience an adventure, they book an exotic package trip. Before they leave, however, they are required to listen to their energy-vampire colleagues making vigorous efforts to talk the trip down: people at your dream beach have been attacked by sharks on more than one occasion. Tourists get robbed by the locals. It's hot in the Caribbean too, too hot. And so on, and so forth. Fortunately, you've now learned what you can do to resist such energy-sucking tirades. "When you have your own planet, you can make your own weather, dear colleague. Until then, it'll be hot in the Caribbean and cold in the Arctic." The dream thieves are killed off practically before they've had a chance to begin.

Diamonds understand adventures as a new kind of growth: seminars abroad, or life-changing experiences such as climbing a mountain. And the superstars? Well, they lead the diamonds in their mountain adventures. For them, there is nothing better than helping others attain diamond status, too.

Write down five adventures that you want to experience:

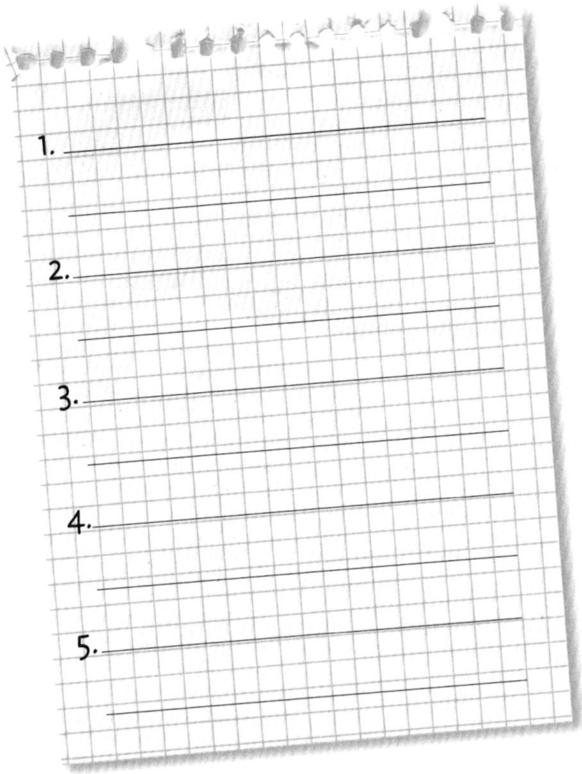

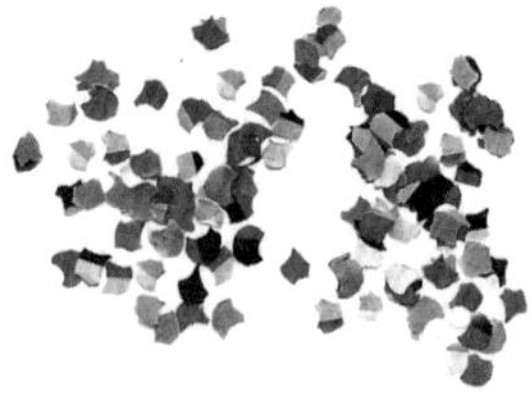

Love and Relationships

Just as with adventure, the definition of "love" varies widely from person to person. In relationships, energy vampires are thoroughly selfish. You almost certainly know of some special couples who are constantly at loggerheads; who call each other "stupid" and "stupider," and make you wonder why they are still together at all. Well, these are energy-vampire couples! Beware of their negativity. And to answer your question: they are together in order not to be alone. They say "I love you" only to hear "I love you" back. Energy vampires also like to equip the bedroom with electronic devices. Instead of shooting wild adventure films with their partner, the energy-vampire couple lie dispassionately side by side and occupy themselves independently with their smartphones or their oversized television.

Less demanding are the ants. Ants approach themselves and their lives in such a systematic manner that they often do not view things as critically as others. Ants tend to have average relationships. When they find someone, their friends often tell them they could have done better.

The only time things become dangerous is when an ant has an energy vampire as a partner. Unfortunately, the biggest threat to our personal development can often be found in our beds. It is particularly dangerous when one partner has elevated themselves from "energy vampire" to "ant" (or "ant" to "diamond") and the other one has no desire to come along with them.

As such, the diamond is much pickier than the ant in their choice of mate. They aren't looking for the "perfect" match, but for someone with whom, at some point, they can change the world. That's exactly what superstars do with their partners: they change the world together, writing books or starting charities. "Neither of us is perfect, but we're perfect for each other." Superstars always keep their relationships fresh. Even those who've been together for years behave the same as the day they met. You might liken it to the way a company treats a newly acquired client. They write love letters, surprise each other, and enjoy each other's personal growth. In short, they stay in phase one of the relationship, and do not slip into routine customer care.

As a quick aside, there's a neat test to find out which stage your relationship is in. Put this book aside, dial the number of your better half and, without any introduction, say the three magical words, "I love you." If all that comes back is, "I love you, too," you know that there is need for action. More appropriate responses could be:

- What's happened?
- Do you need money?
- What have you been up to?
- What are you reading there?

Have you ever been at a seminar where you were asked to do such a thing?

What are you doing to ensure that your relationship remains in the first phase, or to take it back there?

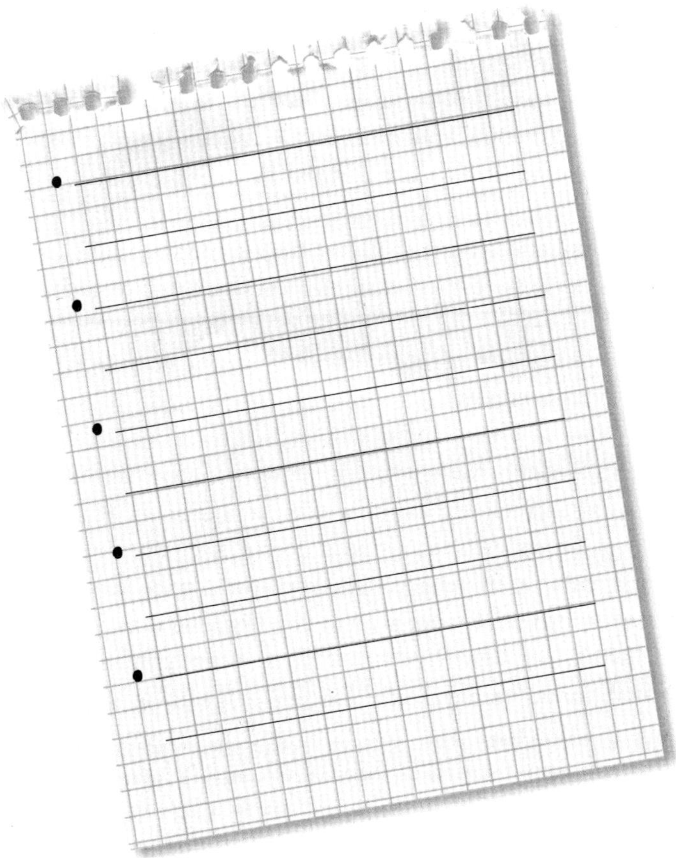

Security

Now we come to a key question, namely, how do we define the word "security"? Energy vampires have a clear stance: for them, the goal is the classic job-for-life. However, since they see this bond as a sort of disruptive factor in their lives, they look for a role in which they are never required to work too much. In interviews, they focus first and foremost on break times and the likelihood of having to work overtime. Work as a passion? Inconceivable. Energy vampires adhere to a clear definition of work as a fundraising effort to afford the things they want—cigarettes, for example. These cigarettes then provide a wonderful excuse for several breaks a day during which energy vampires can talk about their poor working conditions and the niggle in their right-hand side.

Essentially, energy vampires are unable to appreciate their own security because they're too busy complaining about how bad they have it. If the coffee is too weak, it doesn't keep them alert enough to work; if it's too strong, it causes their heart to race. They complain about their bad salary, but are the first to spend a hundred dollars on fireworks for New Year's Eve. They invest primarily in things intended to numb their grief: alcohol, streaming services, and gambling. Above all, they resist any and all change, preferring to stand with a protest sign in front of the factory gates than to take positive action at work. As a result, guess who's going to be first to be laid off when things aren't going so swimmingly? Right—the energy vampire. Even the union won't be able to help them, because companies have these people in their sights from go.

Another tip: any attempt to proselytize to an energy vampire or show them the way out of their mess—through a new business opportunity, for example—is completely futile. They'll always have a thousand reasons why your idea isn't going to work. "I've been working here for twenty-one years, I know what works and what doesn't." Really?

In contrast, when ants speak of security, they're referring to a number of preventative measures. Ants typically pay a certain amount into a savings account each month and have more insurance coverage than they'll ever need. They know exactly when their bus is coming, buy Christmas gifts weeks in advance, and stock up for the holidays ahead of the crowds. The result is that ants are much more relaxed than the rest of their fellow human beings. Ants like to work hard—often in a job where there is a dress code, or where they are required to wear a uniform. This gives them a sense of security. They permit themselves one big annual vacation per year, planned long in advance, or even a small garden. They enjoy a hearty, homely style of luxury.

Diamonds are different again, and derive their security exclusively from a sense of progress. They need the feeling of having taken a step forward each day. Diamonds like to surround themselves with other diamonds, so they can polish and refine each other. Thus strengthened, they constantly look to take on new challenges, such as self-employment. While an energy vampire would be only too keen to reel off the risks, the diamond is not afraid, because their gut tells them what they need to do to ensure their success. They continually evolve, are part of the innovative movement, and are prepared to take risks. They are open to life and to the opportunities it offers. As such, the right environment is the most important factor in a diamond's security.

Superstars have usually suffered several setbacks before they attain superstar status. Because of this, they are not afraid of ups and downs. Like a diamond, a superstar's sense of security is contingent on their environment, which consists of other superstars and diamonds. Superstars know that they will sometimes find themselves in difficult times. Their security is rooted in their ambition to convert more people into diamonds and strengthen their base of mutual support. Often, the superstar is the one to drive social projects, because they are intuitively aware that growth comes from giving back.

Write down five things that give you security:

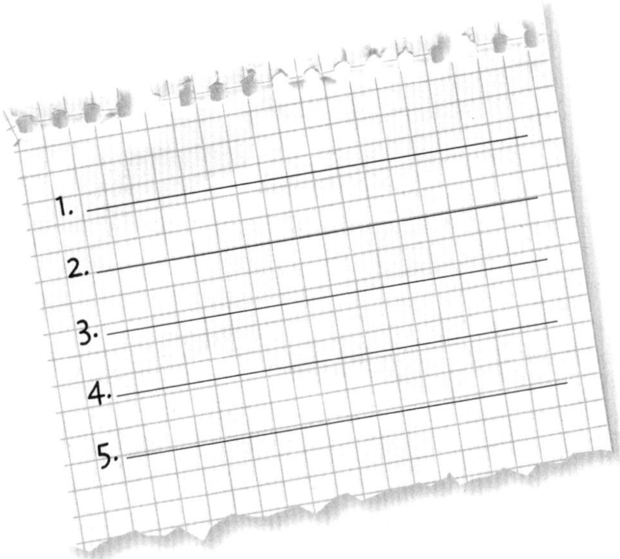

Meaningfulness

Assigning meaning to life or things is a basic pattern of human thinking. When do you, personally, feel that you matter? Again, here, there are clear differences between energy vampires, ants, diamonds, and superstars.

The energy vampire feels a sense of meaning only in very few moments, one of these being group experiences. When they stand in line with other fans at the stadium, wearing the same shirt, and join voices in the team chant, the energy vampire has the feeling of being a tiny link in an important chain. "That's what winners look like," they cry. Personally, I think football and the associated sense of belonging are fantastic. But from an objective point of view, only one party wins, and that's the club. When five thousand people buy a ticket for twenty-five dollars, this means $125,000 for the box office. That's what winners look like, right? When we give meaning to something in our lives or make it meaningful, it gets bigger. I illustrated this earlier, with the idea of a fan that gives oxygen to a fire and makes it bigger. This metaphor fits well here, too.

The ant often perceives its own significance as part of a group with a common interest: at a festival, for example, or at the annual soiree of the community garden association. Often, diamonds perceive their meaning to lie in shared personal development measures, those aimed at their own growth and the growth of others. And the superstar? They organize the adventures of others, and find joy in what results from this. If you want to check out one of the resources that inspires me to keep helping others grow, go to www.youtube.com/soulpancake!

So, we now know the four areas of life that contribute to our happiness. Only when we are satisfied with all of these areas can we finally begin to give something back. As such, I want you to consider how often you are really satisfied. Are you aware of the differences between ants, energy vampires, diamonds, and superstars? What steps do *you* need to take to lead a self-determined and happy life? How many risks are you willing to take for your progress? In a given situation, do you see the opportunity or the risk? How do you intend to make sure that each area is nurtured within your life? This chapter is one of the most important in the book when it comes to really wanting to change something, so take time to think carefully about where you are and where your journey is going to take you. I'll give you a few lines for your notes, and ask you to complete your own wheel of life.

The Wheel of Life

The wheel is divided into the various areas of life:

- Love and relationships
- Adventure
- Security
- Meaningfulness

Middle of the circle = 0 (not present)

Outer edge of the circle = 10 (completely present)

Mark your "Current" status in the individual areas.

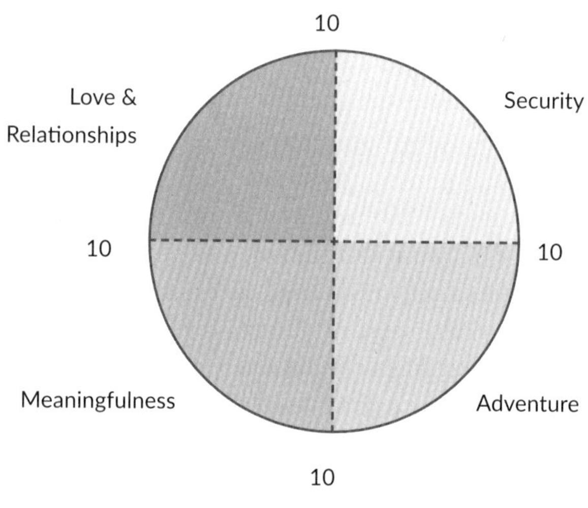

Only when your own life is fulfilled can you give something back to others; only then can the journey toward superstar begin.

Your space for notes on this chapter:

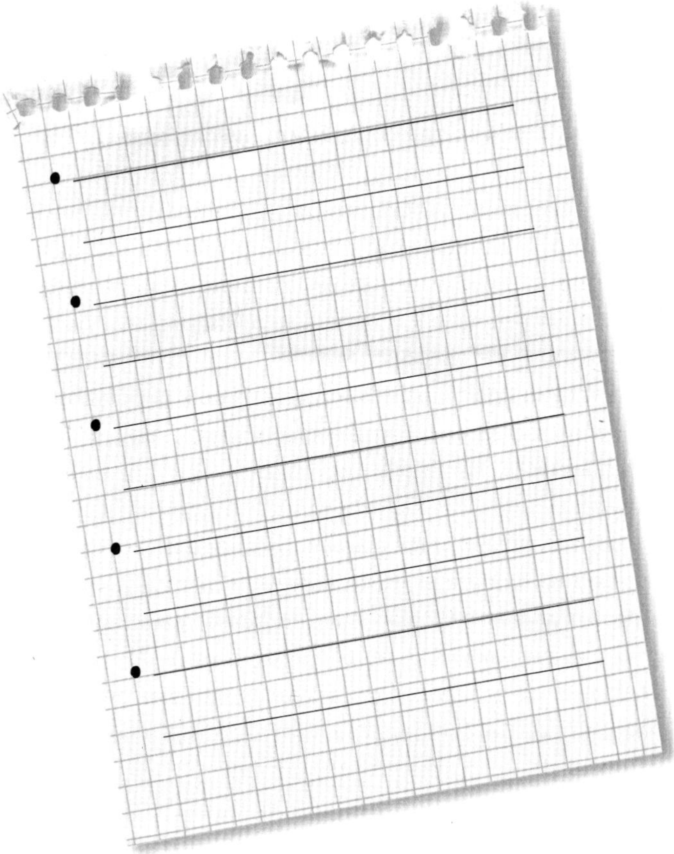

Everything Was Better Before!

Really? I frequently hear people talking very positively about the past, as if they once lived in paradise, or on another planet. Did you know that our brain does this on a completely automatic basis? Over the years, we erase the negative memories and focus only on the beautiful experiences. I see this quite often in my training sessions, when people talk about a past relationship they are simply not able to move beyond. Suddenly, the brain coats everything in a rose-tinted light, and all pain is forgotten. Some even build an altar of photographs, play their favorite shared songs, and smell their ex-partner's T-shirt.

This is not very smart, in my opinion, because our lives are too short to dwell on suffering and waste energy. Incidentally, in the Stone Age, people had no time for such nonsense; life was about bare survival. Negative memories were repressed and positive ones stored. Why? Well, imagine that you are a Neanderthal man and that, upon leaving your cave for hunting, you have a jarring flashback to barely escaping the claws of a predator the day before. This idea would be rather a hindrance, and thus arose the motto of the time: "Eat or be eaten." It is the youngest part of our brain, the prefrontal cortex, that is responsible for this protective mechanism, and I'm glad it exists. At the same time, we all need to live with our pasts; our previous experiences shape us, and they are not to be discussed away. Like battered old cars, we go through the world, inevitably acquiring a few bumps and scratches, but always keeping the engine running. What's more, these scratches are all our own, making us unique and a gift to others.

I fully understand your scratches, and I think that's why we're here. The earth is not built for happiness, but for adventure. All of us walk around with a metaphorical backpack laden with worries, problems, and challenges. You're not alone! It's important to unpack these "stones" and process them, instead of constantly telling everyone how bad you have it. Stop defining yourself by your past. From now on, enjoy every second, because your life is taking place right in the moment, in the here and now. I like to imagine the story of each person in the form of a stock graph. Who decides where the line will go from today? Exactly: you!

Take some time to trace the personal course of life below. Look closely at your curve, your ups and downs. Talk about it with your friends and make sure that from today, the price goes up.

Percentage of Happiness

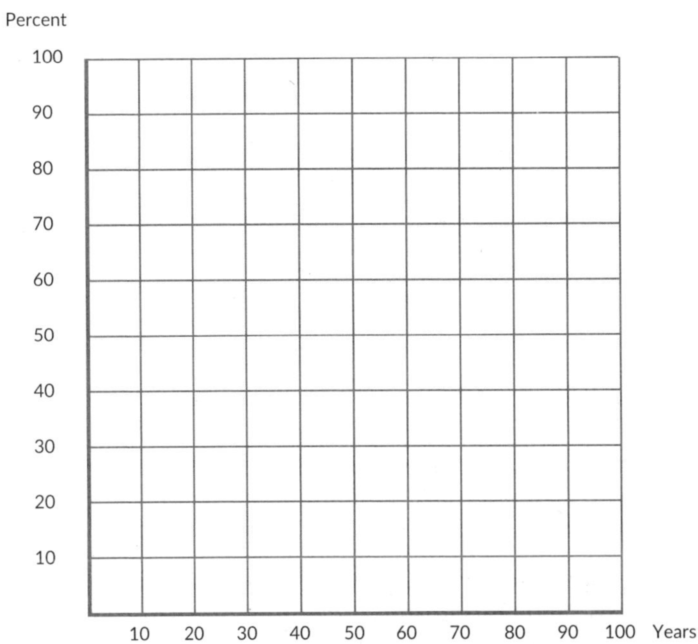

Programming Your Mirror Neurons: A Guide

By now, you've developed the first concrete ideas for your new life. You've been thinking about what your passion and inner motivations could be, and how you define adventure, love, security, and meaning. Now is the time to make a change. There are just four letters that are vital for happiness and success in your life, namely: D-O I-T. Stop thinking about it, stop talking about it. Just do it! Turn around! Surprise those around you with results instead of merely telling them what you intend to do.

In addition, there are a few things in your life I suggest you change completely. Do you remember those little things in your head that attempt to adapt constantly to your environment? Right—your mirror neurons. In order for any intended change to actually work, you must first change the food with which you nourish these nerve cells. Some of the things I'm going to tell you now are minor matters; others may make you say, "How am I supposed to do that? That's just how things are." This is why my first tip for you is to create a vision board. Get a large sheet of paper or poster board, a few magazines, and some scissors and paper, and take some time to focus on yourself and your life. Scour the magazines for pictures that spontaneously appeal to you. How do you imagine your new life, your new self? Where do you live, what do you do, what drives you, what fulfills you, what do you want to achieve?

Cut out all the pictures that make you feel good. The stronger the feeling you associate with an image, the better. Now, stick all the pictures on the sheet and hang it in a place where you'll automatically look at it several times a day. Over your bed, next to your desk, next to the fridge—it doesn't matter, the main thing is that you see it as often as possible. If you travel a lot, take a picture of the poster and put it on your phone as wallpaper. Take the time to look at your vision board several times a day. Feel the energy that each image conveys to you, since this will remind you where you want to go and what your goals are. It will remind you of the importance of even the smallest change, and motivate you to go further. If you have a partner, involve them as much you can in this step. By doing so, you'll always be able to visualize and remember each other's goals.

So, are you ready to reprogram your mirror neurons? Then let's begin.

From my own experience, I can say how brilliantly affirmations can work. In 1999, I wrote myself a letter and set goals for the year 2020. I read through my notes from time to time and have already reached some of these goals today.

Make a few notes of things you know are essential for your vision board:

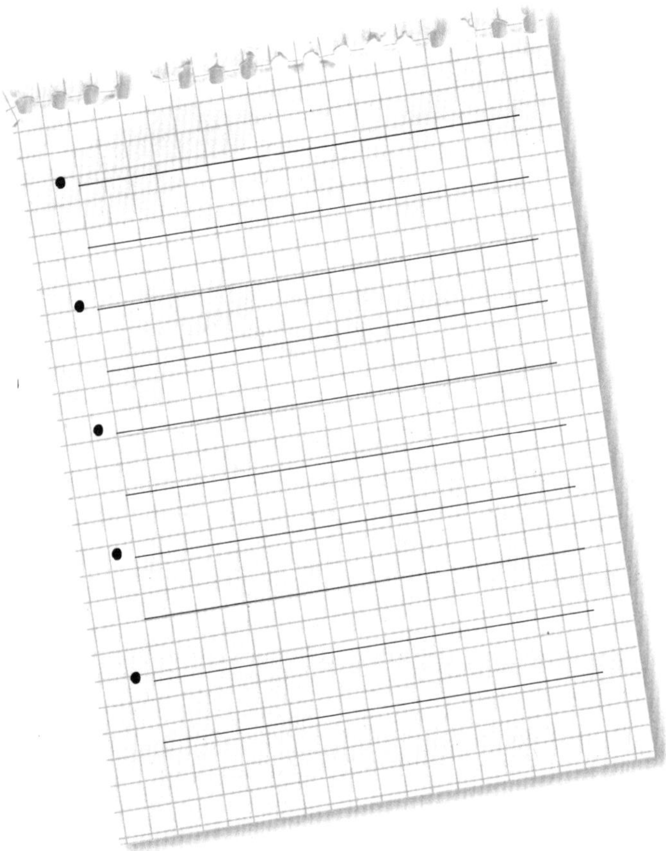

Cut Life-Wasting Words from Your Vocabulary

Question: how many times a day do you use the words "well," "maybe," "normally," "hard to say," "perhaps," "maybe," "possibly," "could have," "would have"?

Know what I call these words? Life-wasters. It may seem drastic, but it's true. Delete these words from your vocabulary and start being specific! How many people do you know who are fundamentally unable to make decisions—who always keep a back door open, whether it's an ice cream flavor, a meeting plan, or a new car?

Now, reflect on how these people affect you. In this context, your brain may spontaneously come upon the names of good friends or pleasant colleagues who, in your eyes, are not energy vampires. Fine. But there's one thing that these people will never be, and that is truly successful. Success and happiness are the result of clear decisions, of daring to do something different. How many items in your everyday life have an enduring place in your heart for the mere fact that they are completely different? Think of your smartphone, your car, your computer. Which big manufacturers come to mind; which ones are really successful? Why is this the case? That's right—because they're different. They made a bold and unambiguous decision to do something different.

This principle applies basically to all successful people. I recommend that you read as many biographies as possible, since this will allow you to discover people who, at a certain point in their lives, decided to be different. Make a decision and stand by it! If it turns out to be wrong, it's not a bad thing: incorrect decisions are what help you grow. Stop talking yourself down and telling lies to yourself and others about why you cannot make it to the top. If your weaker self makes itself felt, tell it to come back another time; its master has a mission.

If you're looking for a piece of advice or an opinion, do you want people to answer you with "well," "hard to say," or "maybe"? No! You ask people you know will be honest. And conversely, even without using "well" or "maybe," you can give honest feedback and avoid being hurtful.

As a final thought on this topic, it's important to stop living in the past and attempting to blame it for your situation in the here and now. Too many people complain time and again that they could be more successful, in love, richer, or otherwise better off if only they had done x, y, or z. The fact is that you cannot change things in your past. Tell the voice in your head that although, yes, it could have been better, it could also have been worse. Stay in the present. This is the only thing you can actively influence—and the best way to do this is by avoiding life-wasting words.

Nourish Your Soul

Question: what do you do when you come home after a long day at work? For millions of people in my native Germany, the choice is clear: they watch TV or gamble online. Now comes one of those suggestions that you're probably going to find crazy: I recommend that you massively restrict your television consumption. Why? Well, TV is the quickest way to squander your resources. Have you ever felt that your thoughts were somehow fogged after a few hours of television consumption? This has even been scientifically proven, with various pieces of research finding that television triggers alpha waves in the human brain. Alpha waves are brain waves between eight and twelve hertz and are commonly associated with relaxed, meditative states of the brain.

While a short stay in this condition is quite advantageous, long periods of television consumption lead to exactly the opposite: an inability to concentrate. If you watch TV for too long, you might as well be staring at a white wall. Is this really the way you want to use your brain? According to Germany's Federal Statistical Office, Germans between the ages of fourteen and sixty-nine watched an average of 220 minutes a day in 2018. Estimates suggest that in 2019 US adults spent an average of three hours and thirty-five minutes watching TV each day.[2] The average American spends as much as twelve hours a day in front of TVs and computers.[3] Is it really a mystery why nobody is able to dream anymore, why people have unlearned how to communicate? People spend hours watching Netflix or Hulu instead of planning a trip for themselves! Couples focus solely on the television and then are surprised that their relationship has suffered—even when the TV is the main event in the bedroom, too!

2 www.statista.com/statistics/186833/average-television-use-per-person-in-the-us-since-2002/

3 www.forbes.com/sites/nicolefisher/2019/01/24/how-much-time-americans-spend-in-front-of-screens-will-terrify-you/#34d7208f1c67

Whole families stay together for hours without talking to each other. The television takes over the conversation. But in this case—and unlike, for example, at school—it's up to you whether you want to participate. I'm not saying you should never watch TV again, but there are two things I highly recommend: firstly, massively reducing your consumption, and secondly—and most importantly—being careful what you watch. Did you know there is such a thing as energy-vampire television, whole programs dedicated to the injustices of the world? Diseases, poverty, the evils of government—all of this is poison for your mind, especially at bedtime.

Have I ever talked about my work in a sleep lab? This was during my psychology studies. There, I encountered countless people who complained of being unable to sleep. Once we had put them into an artificial slumber, the reason for their suffering often became quickly evident: the television. In their troubled sleep phases, patients' dreams simulated horror films, with chainsaws, axes, and physical violence. The lesson of the story? Pay attention to what you watch!

What's more, many programs are intended solely to enable energy vampires to have a little moan the next morning over the first cigarette break with their colleagues. TV offers ample evidence of how terrible the world is—which brings us to another important point, which is to stop watching the news.

You're likely wondering whether I have a screw loose. Isn't it important to know what's happening in the world? Isn't it true that we wouldn't be "educated" otherwise? Believe me, education does not always mean knowing exactly what atrocities are happening outside. Education consists of things that help you grow and give you a sense of well-being. What's more, you'll get to know the really important things from people around you, anyway. Consider these people as your personal filter. Stop filling your brain with unnecessary things. There should be more in your life than TV—so turn it off!

One attractive alternative with which you can occupy your mind in a different and meaningful way is training and books. Remember the wonderful advice I got from a first-class passenger—that anything a person takes in with their eyes and ears will eventually come back out of their mouth? This makes it all the more important for us to nourish our minds with good things. Read books—as many as you can! Read biographies or works on motivation and development. You can find book recommendations on my website at www.tobias-beck.com/booktips, and you'll also find some hints at the end of this book. If you're short on time, you can consume audiobooks on the way to work or to playing sports. Become a pro at making the most of your time for personal development. Listen to podcasts! These are lots of audio episodes with experts willing to pass on their knowledge completely free of charge.

You'll see amazing results after 365 days if you devote just one hour a day to investing in yourself. If you embrace and follow all the rules, you'll quickly achieve an MBA: a "massive bank account." Incidentally, I personally like to further my education in the form of seminars where, unlike at school or university, I can purchase niche knowledge that is offered and taught by people who've achieved exactly what I want to do. According to my tax adviser, I've invested about $250,000 in personal development since 1998. Why? Because nobody can ever take that away from me. Note, however, that personal training does not have to be expensive; there are lots of great courses to be found free of charge online.

- TED: www.ted.com
- EDX: www.edx.org
- tobias-beck.com/en/bewohnertest

Another advantage is that, when attending these types of personal development events, you'll meet people who click in the same way as you do. You'll meet people with whom you can talk about your interests. Nowhere else will you have the chance to meet so many diamonds in one fell swoop. Connect with these people and listen to their stories. Does this not sound more exciting than a program you've already seen several times over? Seminars also give the best chance of meeting personal mentors—people who will elevate you into the next category. Organize mastermind meetings with people in your city. (I, for example, take regular ski trips with my mastermind group.) After a few descents, we sit down together and make plans about how to change the world. Believe me, there's no better way to grow your horizons and your ability to dream big than to surround yourself with diamonds and superstars. Moreover, it makes perfect sense to engage with people from different industries and with very different worldviews, because you can learn from them, too. Pay attention to who you interact with; otherwise, you'll end up vacationing solely with other versions of yourself, and that makes no sense at all from a development perspective.

Make sure to spend time reading regularly. The first fifteen minutes after waking up, a few minutes right after work, the last half-hour before going to sleep—it doesn't matter the time of day. Protect some space. See books for what they are: the chance to absorb the valuable knowledge of an expert at a reasonable price. If you concentrate fully on this feeling, you'll appreciate each line that much more.

Set an Example

Know those days when everything is just going badly? Where you need a coffee the second you get out of bed? Where the radio plays the wrong songs, the people in the street annoy you, and you long for peace and quiet? Mentally insert yourself, briefly, into one of these days. How do you present yourself? How do you deal with others? How do you respond to colleagues when they ask for things? How do you greet your family at the end of the day?

Note down some of the thoughts you have on such days:

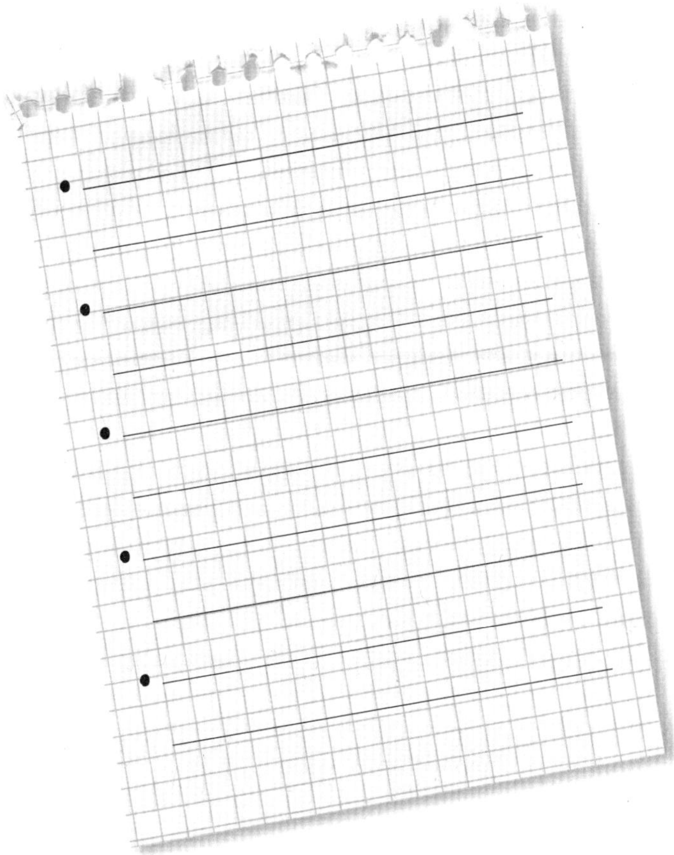

Such miserable days are dominated by your "lower self." Of course, the lower self also has a counterpart: your "higher self." On the days when the higher self dominates, you feel like embracing the whole world and spending time engaging with others and their interests. Even though you might be stuck in a traffic jam, you sing along loudly to every song on the radio. Your favorite food is waiting you at home, and despite the rain, the sun is shining. Know what I mean?

Reflect briefly on the thoughts and feelings you experience on such days:

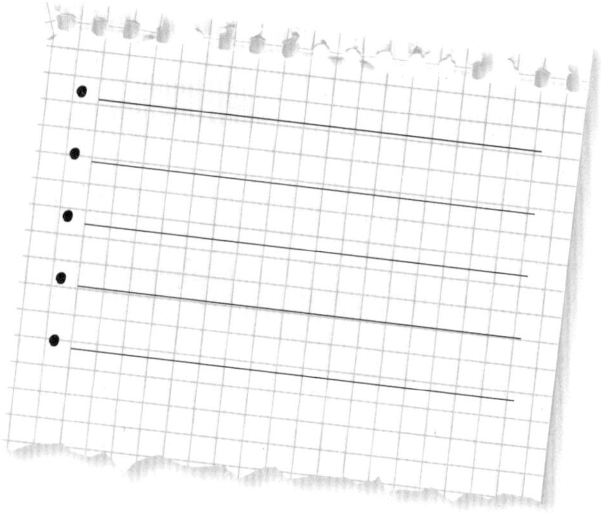

At this point, I have a wild-sounding suggestion for you. What would you say to making a pact with yourself—namely that, starting today, you promise to be the best version of yourself *every single day*. Yes, I'm serious! Just think: would it not be incredible to experience a little more of your "higher self" with each day that goes by?

"How might this work?" you might be thinking. Well, by starting on a small scale. Even if you're stuck in the lower self, you have the power to decide how long to stay there. My suggestion is to take a photo of the notes you made above and read them through in the moments when you feel the lowest. Decide whom you want to radiate: the lower self you described, or the higher one.

Read them out loud, then decide. Then, begin with small actions: let the family with the children go ahead of you in a long line, and watch the reactions. Smile at the person on the street and see what you get back. Play your favorite CD if the radio is annoying you. Take yourself out of the hustle and bustle of life for a moment and enjoy the daisy that's growing in the middle of the street. Appreciate the wonders of everyday life!

One more thing: being the best version of yourself is especially important if you have children. They have high sensitivity and will notice immediately if you are in a "lower self" state. In this state, we say things we do not mean, but that can nevertheless trigger lots of emotions in our kids. "Don't be annoying!" "You can't do that!" "You're not smart enough!" "Don't be such a wimp!"

Do you remember these sentences emanating from your parents' mouths? What effect did they have on you? Partners, friends, and family can easily become victims of our lower self. As such, you need to make a conscious decision—for yourself and your environment. In many situations, both inner voices will come to the fore and compete for attention. Be mindful when giving a tip at the restaurant; more specifically, if the service was good, give the amount that comes to mind immediately upon seeing the bill. It is not the rationalizing voice that should prevail in this decision. If you receive a bill for eleven dollars, follow your gut and leave a twenty. See what chain of events you trigger. The universe works with the Law of Resonance. Just as bad attracted bad with the seagull story, you'll attract goodness if you do good.

Stop Comparing Yourself to Others

If you really want to be happy in life, it's important to stop constantly comparing yourself to others. Envy and resentment will hinder you from succeeding, because you're focusing your energy on what you do not have. This is the wrong approach. You might have heard of the Law of Attraction, which states that you receive the things you focus on. That's why I suggested you create a vision board: to help you narrow down what you really want and what really brings you joy.

This is also why energy vampires are neither happy nor successful, because their focus is solely on what is bad. In plain English: if you genuinely believe you have no chance of promotion, that's the way it will actually be. If you genuinely believe you'll never reach your desired weight, your next trip will inevitably be to the fast food restaurant. If you're convinced that you are unfortunate, life will give you lemons. You get what you believe in! And that belief will not change if you constantly compare yourself with others.

What have we learned? What are the things that trigger change in our lives? Right! Desire or pain—and our passion to find what really drives us. Each day, we must celebrate the things we have and direct our energy toward the things we want. Envy and frustration deplete this energy. If friends and acquaintances achieve something, we should rejoice with them. We should celebrate their progress toward the next level. At the same time, we can feel happy that we have such people around us. Remember: you are the sum of the five people you spend the most time with. What this means for you is that, if these people get ahead, you can, too. Isn't that great? Incidentally, no matter what you do, you will always find people who rank "above" and "below" you. That's why comparing yourself makes no sense at all.

Become the Superstar of Your Own Life and Give Something Back

Ask yourself what you personally give back in your life. Can you imagine anything greater than changing the lives of those around you for the better every day? Truly effecting change—and by doing what you love? Many people are too driven by what makes them happy, or at least what they *think* makes them happy: money and/or a powerful job. If you take time to look closely at "successful" people, you'll see many of them appear like robots. I know some individuals with millions in the bank. Does this make them happy? No. Interestingly, while studies show that people who earn more than $75,000 a year have a greater sense of happiness than peers who earn less, anything beyond that will not necessarily have an effect. Many top earners are stuck in a system they cannot escape. They hide behind a mask of consumption and bought "happiness." But do they know the joy of giving something back?

Dare to stand by your wishes and discover who you really are. Free yourself from the expectations of others and think about what truly drives you. What experiences have you had? Which bridges have you crossed? Which tribulations have you overcome? What characterizes you in your dealings with others? With what kind of people do you wish to surround yourself?

Above all, how can you help others and give something back?

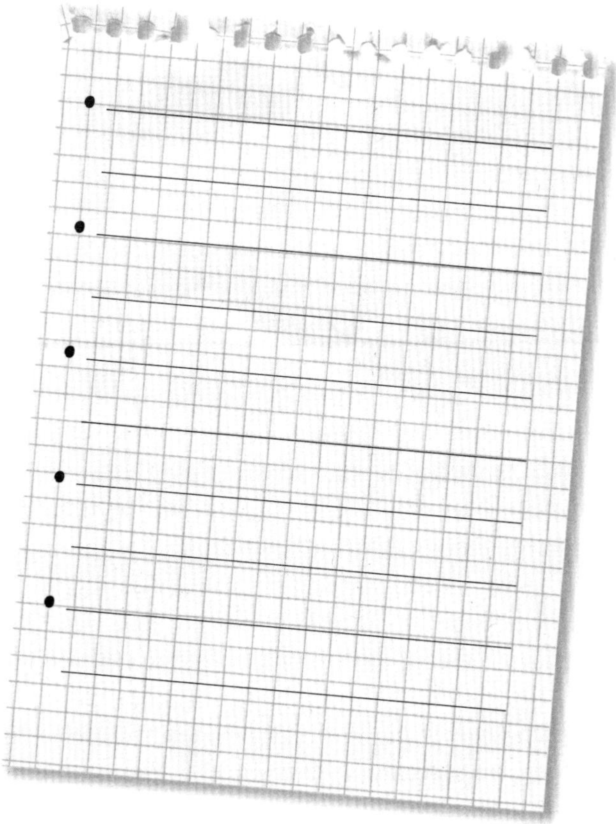

What's the Point of It All?

In this chapter, I'll explain why it is so important for you to achieve your goals and send clear messages to those around you about things you do and do not like. I want to give you the strength to speak up when you don't want something, and to make your desires known. As a child and adolescent, I had very painful experiences of what it is like when someone tries to break the will of another.

It all started harmlessly, when my mother was looking for a kindergarten spot for my little sister in the summer of 1988. I was eleven, and remember vividly the endless waiting times in the overheated car as we drove around to every place in Wuppertal. We received only rejections. One day, however, the tide turned: my sister was given a place in a private play group, and I was to join her after school for homework assistance. That seemed a good idea considering my bad grades—at least, that's what I thought at the time.

To make a long story short, we were slowly and unconsciously drawn into one of the worst sects in Germany to date. Hopefully, everything I'm about to tell you will give you some idea of why I never intend to be silenced again. In retrospect, it is a mystery to me how adults and educated people could participate in such practices. After a short time, our whole life was in the "church," and harmless Bible lessons became a perfidious construct that had little to do with the normal, "outside" world.

Although I was still permitted to go to a public school, I was forbidden to interact with my classmates. While other children were reading *Bravo* magazine and watching television, for me, such things were vilified and punished. I was punished particularly frequently back then, since even as a child, I didn't like being told what to do.

One day, when I was caught watching television, I was threatened with a thing I had long dreaded. Every Sunday, "sinners" were led before the church and publicly humiliated. They were placed on a platform and illuminated with a spotlight to enable all of the two or three hundred members to shout at them for hours until they confessed their "sins" and begged for mercy. Finally, my turn had come. These ceremonies were always performed in the absence of family members, so I couldn't hope for any backup.

I kicked my legs all the way there, biting and lashing out with my hands and feet. Tears ran down my face. It was futile. I sat in a chair, in the bright spotlight, and endured the shouting. Finally, I promised not to sin again, and was handcuffed to a wooden house in the garden to reflect on my "sins." I would love to forget about this lengthy and terrible time—but instead of complaining daily about the claustrophobia that has plagued me since, I have taken advantage of my past. I transformed my grief and frustration into anger, which ultimately led to my life's purpose: I want to help others grow, so that they never have to experience what I did.

Back then, I found it especially terrifying to see the female church members walk around in their headscarves on Sundays and communicate in their own language: the "Language of Angels," which consisted solely of clicking sounds. The memory still gives me nightmares. The prospect of marriage was similarly dreadful, with men and women being married off at the direction of the "leadership" regardless of whether they liked each other. A potato sack was placed over their heads, and when it was lifted, their new life partner would be standing in front of them. Some children were locked up with water and bread in an attempt to break their will, but after my public humiliation, I was spared this ordeal.

It was not until my parents were about to divorce—when my father refused to pay a quarter of his income to the sect each month—that everyone came to their senses. We cut the cord. Weeks later, strange cars parked in the driveway and the phone rang off the hook—all in an effort to get us back. Following that horrible time, I had zero self-confidence, and my self-image was a disaster. I was afraid to enter into relationships with others, to permit closeness, because I was worried about being hurt again. Today, I've learned to accept my past as a gift, and as part of my personal story. We're all here to learn, and back then, I learned a lot.

Note down some negative situations from your past that have helped to shape who you are:

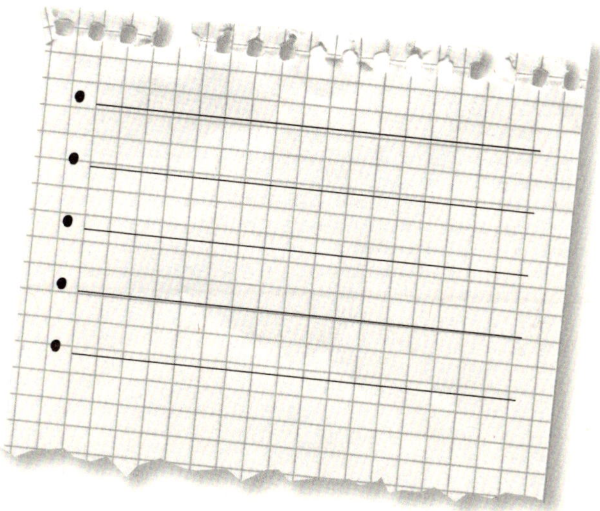

What did you learn from these situations?

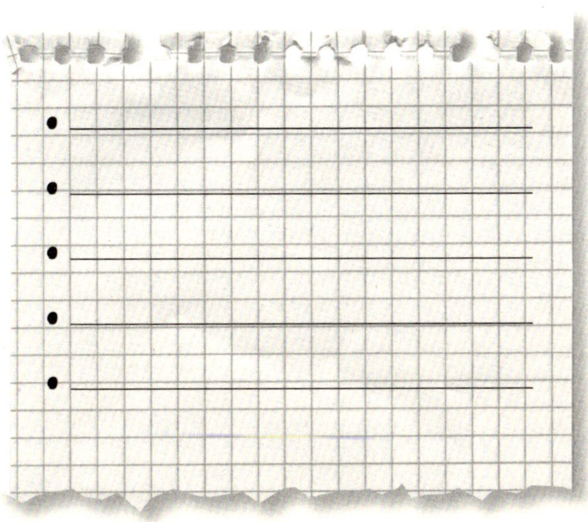

What are the difficult situations in your life that have made you strong?

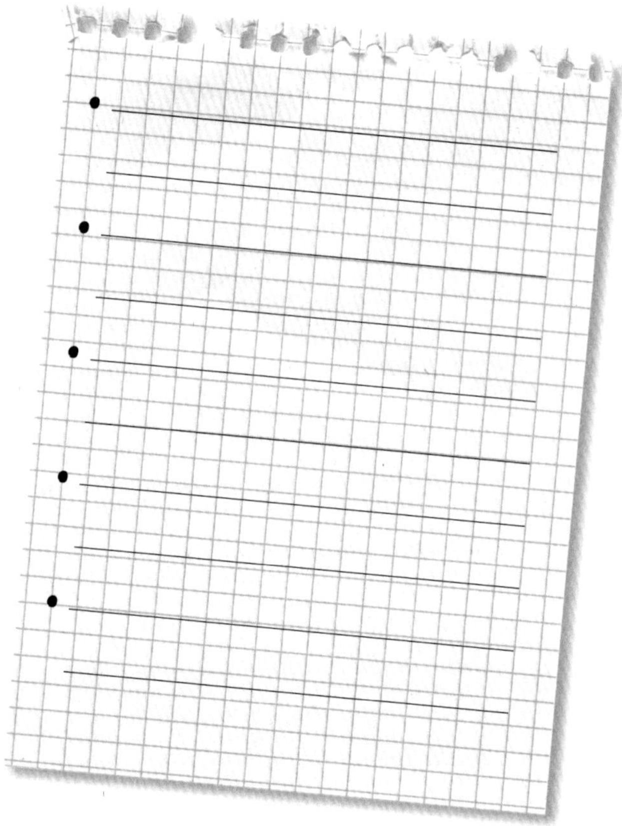

Don't Ask for Permission

You are the captain of your life, and neither your childhood home, your education, nor anything else in the past is responsible for your success. This also means that you do not need to ask for permission to live your dreams. All successful people are doers, not thinkers. To become self-employed, for example, you need a great business idea, a willingness to work on your dream consistently, and a business license. That's about it. When I started out, I didn't ask anyone whether it would make sense to hold public seminars or to record my anti-energy-vampire podcast. The moment you ask others, you are boycotting your project yourself.

Why? Well, take my public seminars as an example. If I'd asked people for advice, many of them would likely have said, "Tobi, there are so many seminars available, and your corporate seminars are going well." At that point, my thoughts would already have been moving in the wrong direction. Without their advice, however, I was totally free—and almost exploded inwardly with enthusiasm as I thought about how many lives could be changed. A similar thing happened with the podcast. Yes, I knew there were many already; but I bought the equipment and started anyway, without asking anyone. What happened? We immediately took first place in the business category! The golden rule is: don't talk and discuss at length, but simply do. Our seminars and products eventually ended up grossing millions of dollars. Whose place was it to give permission for that? The universe, parents, friends? Never make your success dependent on others; in that case, you can only lose. If I'd listened to the stories that were fired at me from all sides, I'd still be watching life from the bench.

To give you the kick you need each day, I want to share my personal "declaration." Read over these lines as many times as you need to program your subconscious mind for success. For best results, do it standing, with a loud voice and your hand on your heart:

- I am a winner
- I am true to myself
- I add value to others' lives
- I am enough
- I am loved
- I am a winner
- I strive for growth
- I give 100 percent in every situation
- I am a problem solver
- I do what I love
- I am a winner
- I give back
- I motivate others
- I inspire others
- I trust my inner voice
- I am a winner, and I love my life

Your Personal Environment and Your Growth

A lot of dangers lurk on the path of personal development, and the greatest is deeply rooted within you. One of the most difficult challenges you'll face is dealing with the opinions and comments of others. All of us want to be loved and respected—and above all, we need attention and appreciation for what we do. Often, we look for these things in our personal environment. After attending a seminar or practicing the insights we've gained from an interesting book, we look for the reactions of our friends, relatives, and colleagues. Unfortunately, often, they laugh at what we are doing, or completely deny us recognition. If you used to be happy to drink yourself into oblivion, but no longer want to traipse around the bars with your drinking buddies, what do you think their reaction will be? "Yes, it's great that you're starting to live your dream"? If you're waiting for this sentence, you'll be waiting a long time, because those around you will try with all their might to pull you back into old patterns. This negative effect can take hold in even the closest of families.

Some years ago, I received a call that disturbed me very much. The father of a young seminar participant had called up to berate me. Upon speaking to him, I remembered his son, Flausen. I inquired further. Shaking with rage, the man told me of the change in his offspring since he'd attended my Masterclass of Personality. As far as the father was concerned, it was impudent to speak of "life dreams." He'd just secured his son an apprenticeship in his company, where he was bound to work for at least the next twenty years. Now, the son wanted to become an artist. "What an ungainful occupation," the man said, hanging up in rage.

This call played on my mind. The father loved his son, no doubt, or he would not have become so emotional. Only when something is close to our hearts do we permit our emotions to run so high. On the other hand, the reason for the call was sad. When someone begins to grow internally and achieve measurable results, the people around them start to feel fear: the fear of no longer being enough. I observe this feeling even with parents. Although they basically want the best for their children, if the offspring begin to outstrip them in success, the relationship can fall apart—as with the angry father on the phone.

One thing that I consider especially important is to be sensitive to those around you. Don't preach: go your own way, and let people go theirs. I've made many mistakes in this regard, and lost people who were dear to me through ill-considered behavior. I wanted to proselytize to all, became arrogant, and began to lose touch with reality. I was too rabid in my choice of words, and for a long time, I could not understand why everyone didn't want the same things as me. But this isn't reality. Many people simply lack the strength to read books that force them to engage with themselves and their choices.

I've now stopped coaching my circle of friends and acquaintances, and only offer help when asked. Why? Well, I want the people around me to feel comfortable, not like they have something to prove. Instead of preaching, I ask a lot of questions and look for the positive aspects of my counterparts' characters instead of merely judging them. For Christmas, I give books that open the door to the world of personality development. If someone says they like what they read, I smile and invite them to our public seminars. At this point, the reactions are often positive. "Why haven't I thought about these things earlier?" they ask. "Because you've only become open to them now, my friend," I think to myself. "Welcome to my world."

The Magic Aquarium

Once a year, when I was a little boy, we received a visit from my uncle from the US. He was a tall, stocky man with a gray beard and a friendly nature, and he was the star of our family. As a young adult, he left Germany, became a millionaire in New York, and was a master at telling stories. These often revolved around successful people. We recorded a few on tape, and still listen to them at family celebrations today. I remember how we were mesmerized by his words when he told of the big wide world. He liked to read books on personality development, and he was an early believer in the power of positive psychology.

For us children, in particular, my uncle always had very special lessons. He often came to visit over Christmas, when the Christmas tree shone bright in the living room and the house was filled with the scent of German cooking. My uncle looked forward to it the whole year long. I, too, was always excited, because he brought very special gifts. None of my friends received anything similar.

So I stood before the Christmas tree as a five-year-old boy on Christmas Eve and, as we sang the obligatory songs, my eyes alighted on a parcel with my name. In my mind's eye, I envisioned a remote-controlled car or something equally spectacular. In a few seconds' time, it would be in my hands! I tore off the paper and stared blankly at the contents: an aquarium for children. I looked up. Before I could complain, he said, "Tobi, I'm not going to give you the presents you want, but rather those that will help you in life." I didn't understand anything, and I was sorely disappointed.

The next day, we drove to the city to buy a fish from a pet store. "It's time to take responsibility for things in your life," my uncle told me, "and a fish will be the first step." Every day, after kindergarten, I was to feed it, and if I noticed any change, I was to call America. "Horst," the goldfish, moved into our home. At first, I dutifully attended to his needs, but soon I lost the will to continue. Soon, it was my mother who was feeding him and changing his water.

Summer passed and school started—a dramatic chapter in my life. Even in my first year, I realized how difficult it would be to adapt. I rebelled against my teacher, who informed me daily how stupid I was. I came home sad, cried often, and had my parents at a loss. Autumn passed, then winter. My uncle's annual visit drew closer. As usual, I stood at the window and looked forward to seeing him and hearing his stories.

This time, he lifted a gigantic package out of the car trunk and placed it under the Christmas tree. I couldn't wait to open it. Now, surely, my wish would have been granted! I saw the remote-controlled car in my mind's eye.

As I unwrapped the package, my uncle stood behind me. "Remember, Tobi, I'll always give you the things you *need* in life, not those you want." I stared blankly at the contents of the package. Another aquarium?! This one was bigger, more colorful, and full of accessories. I stamped an angry foot on the floor. "I already have an aquarium, and the goldfish just swims in it!"

Tears of disappointment ran down my face. "Come on," my uncle said. We went to my room, sat down on the bed, and talked. Even today, more than thirty-four years later, I remember the conversation well.

"Your parents told me you've had problems adjusting to school. It was like that for me, for a long time. I even had problems adapting in Germany—that's why I went to New York, where everything is bigger, more colorful, and brimming with possibilities." It was not until much later that I realized what this meant; that we were in the middle of one of life's most important lessons. We set up the big aquarium in my room. "Listen to me, Tobi. Horst is moving to a much larger house, with more space. Take care of him. You must learn to take responsibility for others. Every day, when you come home from school, check on Horst, and if you notice anything, call me in New York."

Days and weeks went by, and I checked on my roommate each day after school. One day, I noticed something: Horst had grown significantly! I went into the living room, dialed my uncle's number, and told him about my discovery. "Tobi, take good care of yourself," he said. "Everything in the world is programmed for growth; however, we can only grow as much as our environment and our home permit. Horst was not able to grow in the small pond, but now he has room to blossom. Whenever you notice that your aquarium is getting too small, jump into a larger one. When you realize you're the biggest fish, jump out and go somewhere bigger." At the time, I didn't understand a word—but his final metaphor still stays with me.

"What's the greatest creature in the ocean, Tobi?" he asked.

"The whale?"

"Right, my young friend. The whale lives in the expanse of the ocean, since there, it has room to grow." It was to be our last conversation, because that same year, my uncle died. It was not until much later that I realized the meaning of his stories. He was interested in my personal growth, not my short-term enthusiasm for a remote-controlled car. The aquarists and fish experts among you will tell me that Horst would not have thrived in either aquarium—but I assure you, he did!

The Parachute

Imagine you're standing on the ridge of a gigantic mountain, with a parachute on your back. You look down and can barely see the valley below. Fear and doubt start to rise: your stomach cramps, your mouth becomes dry, and you notice a huge lump in your throat. Your entire body begins to shake. "What if the parachute doesn't open?" says your inner voice. "What if I hurt myself on the jump and hit the rock face?" These are the voices of all those who have sought to keep you small, forcing you to do things that don't fit your plan. These voices supply the negative ideas that make your inner child and inner flame ever smaller and weaker:

- You can't do that!
- Better a bird in the hand than two in the bush! What makes you so special that you think you can break the mold?
- You're too tall, too small, too fat, too thin, too old, too young, too un-athletic...

Even as these sentences buzz through your head, aggressive, like a swarm of hornets, something magical happens. You hear another voice, quiet and incomprehensible at first: "You have to jump." For many years, that voice has been suppressed. Not anymore. You take the grief and pain of your life and turn it into power and anger. Every muscle of your body, every fiber, every cell, is ready to take the leap of your life.

You take a step forward and another deep breath. Far away, you still hear the warnings of others on the path, groaning about the ascent under the weight of heavy backpacks. But your inner power is greater. Your inner child has broken free of the shackles that bound it for so many years. It is no longer prepared to make itself small; rather, it has torn down the concrete walls and its flame is burning bright. It grows bigger and bigger. In your eyes burns the desire to make a masterpiece of your life. Like a fireball, these forces combine. You put aside your last doubt and jump.

Before you know it, you're heading for the abyss. You couldn't have foreseen this, not by any stretch of the mind. Instead of the euphoria you expected, the wind catches you and throws you against the sharp rocks. You hit your leg, bleed, cry out in pain, and wish you hadn't jumped. But the freefall goes further. As the world rushes past, you become frightened of your own courage. At this altitude, there is no one to catch you. Again, your body is smashed against the rock face.

You scream, you question everything—and suddenly, you hear a loud noise. You're dragged upward, as if by a magical hand. Your parachute has opened! You're flying—and it's the flight of your life. Nature is at your service. The wind that once caused you pain is now providing buoyancy.

As you float, you see the beautiful landscape from a different perspective. Next to you, an eagle glides in circles and gives you a glance—a glance that says that you are like-minded. Suddenly, you have the feeling you've been searching for. You're free, happy, and full of strength. The experts call this "flow." Enjoy this new power, because you're now able to retrieve it at the push of a button. This is the leap of your life. No one can help you, and no one will. What's more, no one can give you permission—not your parents, the state, or your friends or relatives, especially not those who have not jumped themselves.

In summary, I implore you: no matter how old you are or how great your fear is, jump at least once in your life. Ask all the people who dared, and they'll tell you with smiles about what happened afterward.

You Are Not an Accident

After this chapter, you might think I'm completely crazy, enlightened, or simply a dreamer. Perhaps there's something to the idea that there are no coincidences in life, and everything follows a plan.

In my keynote speeches, I like to start with simple, imaginative examples from the animal kingdom as a basis for later drawing parallels with humans. There's the story of the little bee, for example, who spies the light of day in a green meadow and continuously pursues its destiny. What is the nature of this destiny? Well, in insects, everything is genetically programmed. The bee simply follows its plan, with no need for independent will. It leaves the hive every morning to search for the most fragrant flowers. It's lucky: the next meadow isn't far, and it flies eagerly from flower to flower. Why does it do this? The bee doesn't know; it simply brings home pollen every day for its family to turn into honey.

The bee has small barbs on its legs, designed for the pollen to stick to. Does it know this? No, it simply pursues its purpose. It is even less aware that this supposedly aimless flight is what makes our entire ecosystem and life on earth possible. It just spreads its wings and takes off every day. Can this really be coincidence? The barbs, the pollen, the pollination, and our ecosystem? Much more exciting is the question of your own role in the universal plan. Personally, I don't believe in coincidences. If the bee can make such a major contribution, what could we achieve if, as conscious people, we finally break free of our mental chains?

My question to you is: what do you find easy, and what would you do if you didn't have to earn any money? Which meadows would you fly over?

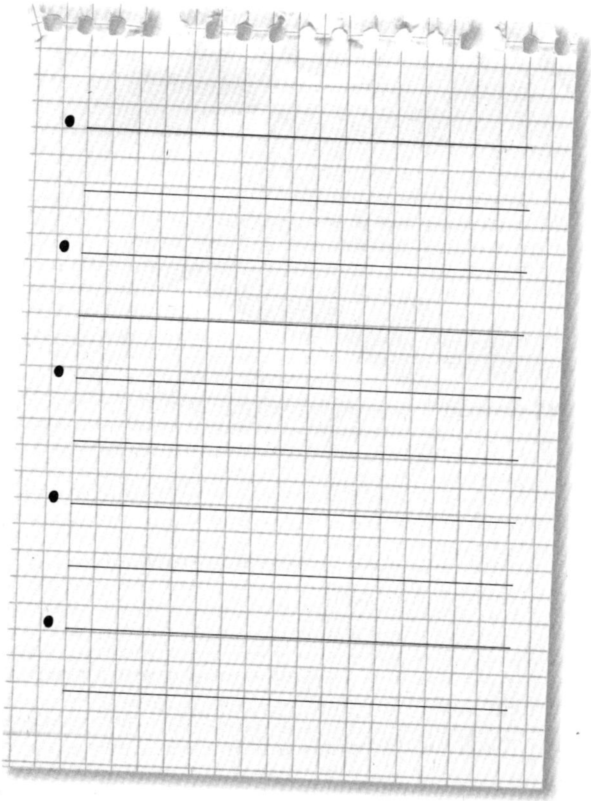

What did you love doing when you were at school?

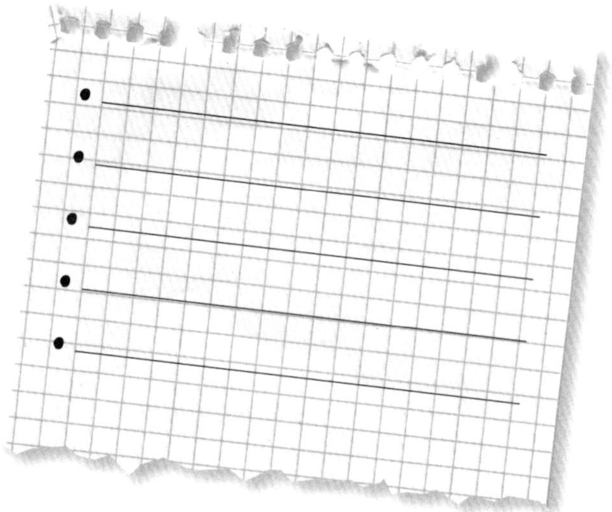

In my seminars, I'm often asked how we are supposed to decide what we are destined to do. The answer to this is quite simple: by ceasing to search for our happiness in the outer world and seeking out the inner self. Our inner navigation system—or, more accurately, our subconscious—constantly attempts to remind us what we should or should not do in the form of emotions. At the same time, external influences affect us greatly, and we are constantly bombarded with supposedly good advice. In the end, all great teachers in history were simply doing what their inner voice told them. We should emulate them. If we do, all the doors of life will open. We'll find ourselves in worlds we never knew existed.

Do you really believe that Thomas Edison asked for permission to invent the light bulb? Did Bill Gates and Mark Zuckerberg appeal to the family council for the approval of their projects, or did they call the computer experts? No one can help more or be a better adviser than you, because no one has yet achieved the things that lie within you. Your hopes and dreams are so unique to you that there's only one proof of them all being connected: your success!

Incidentally, your inner voice is simultaneously also your biggest enemy, because its primal aim is to deter you from adventure and keep you safe. Since the dawn of time, we as organisms have been programmed for survival and safety. When our ancestors left the cave, they were punished by violent reactions, by thoughts of "fight or flight." This is essentially still the case. As soon as you stand in front of a group and venture your life idea, you enter a state of discomposure that makes you sweat, feel sick, and go red in the face.

I've experienced firsthand what it's like to stand up for your own ideas. Believe me, I'm no different from you. I'm afraid, I'm unsure, and I've experienced tons of sleepless nights. Particularly when I summoned the courage to say what I thought and where I wanted to go, I was exposed to the scorn of the masses. To this day, many friends have not understood that I did not discover my passion until my mid-twenties; that I no longer want to go to clubs and numb my pain with alcohol. "Who do you think you are?" and "Why should we listen to you?" are things I've heard often. But instead of letting these barbs bring me down, I use them as a driving force. What counts in the end is not the prophecies of those around you, but only what you achieve.

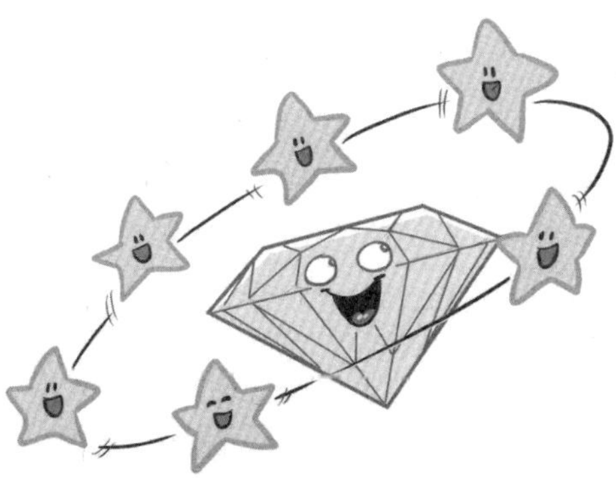

What helps a lot is to travel to the places where great personalities did their work. Look at the surroundings and feel the energy. I am especially grateful for my travels to Calcutta, where I volunteered in the children's homes set up by Mother Teresa. She is one of the biggest superstars in history. Instead of accepting the status quo and regretting the situation of the poor, she built homes and took children off the streets.

We need to listen much more frequently to our built-in navigation systems, because intuition is the best guide for our lives. Just as animals intuitively sense natural catastrophes and behave accordingly, we, too, can allow ourselves to be guided by our inner voices. Unfortunately, many people have completely paralyzed their inner voices by consuming alcohol, nicotine, or other drugs.

Diamonds Are Created Under Pressure—Just Like You!

In nature, nothing happens on a whim. If a big tree stands in the forest for hundreds of years and is suddenly brought down by bad weather, is it gone? No—the opposite! It rots. Bit by bit, nature carries it under the ground. At some point, after many years of pressure, something new is created: coal. When more pressure is added to coal, a diamond results. More generally, any particle exposed to a certain level of external pressure will eventually be unable to endure it any longer, and something new will be born.

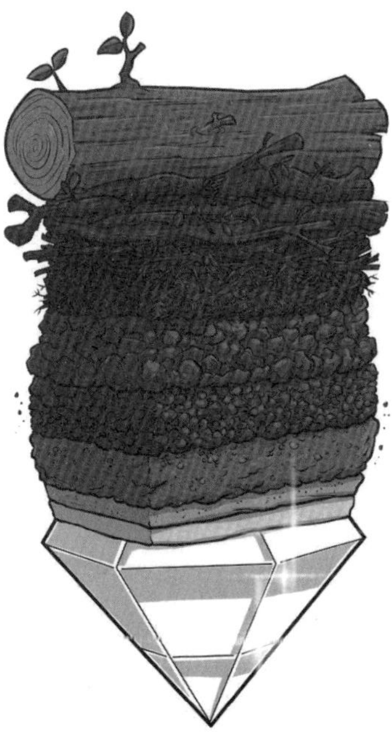

This simple concept has completely changed my life. Nowadays, I deliberately place myself in immensely pressured situations so that something new, amazing, and creative can arise. What does this have to do with you and your life? Well, most people I know spend their entire lives avoiding pain and pressure for the fear that something bad might happen. To learn how to master the sails of life, I believe we must enter the storm—because only on the high seas can a captain learn to keep a ship on course under even the most adverse conditions.

The above is why I often try to attend seminars that take me to my personal limits. Two years ago, I was asked to attempt, blindfolded, to evade a fighter at a workshop in Malaysia; this was to help me trust my intuition. Despite my panic and sweaty hands, I experienced firsthand how incredibly powerful our inner compass is. When you test your limits, you have to be ready for one thing: the moment the hormones flood your body, your intelligence decreases radically and you can no longer think logically. In short: emotions up, intelligence down. Be prepared!

In my life, there have been many situations where I felt I could no longer stand the pressure. I used to believe myself to be living in perfect happiness. Only later did I realize that I was actually in the midst of a great adventure—and one I could only partially influence. This challenging life is about finding out what is hidden inside us.

What situations can you recall in your life in which the pressure was almost too much to bear?

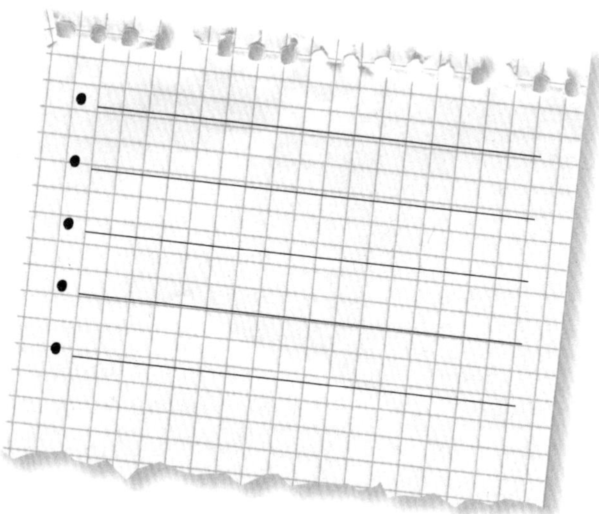

What resulted from these situations?

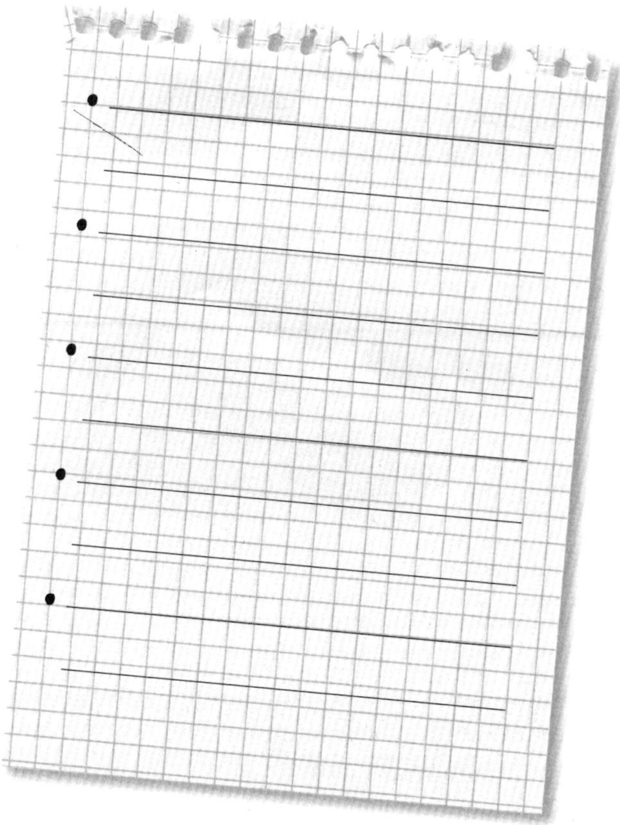

The Dalai Lama and the Great "*Mimimi*"

Some time ago, the Dalai Lama held an audience in the Centennial Hall in Frankfurt, and I was allowed to attend. I was very much inspired by his presence. I'm a firm fan of thinking outside the box, which meant that, when he suggested moving the NATO headquarters to Moscow, he already had me mesmerized.

The best part, however, was the question and answer session. "Can you pray for the people of the world?" the first participant said. His question was loaded with hidden implications.

The lama's answer surprised me very much and, at the same time, completely confirmed my positive impression. He paused for a moment. "Yes, I can pray," he replied, "but that's no use, and has never been of any use." The audience was stunned. The lama then went on to tell a story. Some time ago, the economy in a certain region had begun to blossom after his visit. Years later, he returned, and the governor of the region thanked him for all he had done with his prayers. At that moment, the Dalai Lama began to laugh like a child. "The governor and his people did everything," he said. "I just made them believe they could do it."

Then came my personal aha moment. A woman came to the microphone, her face marked by grief, and immediately began to bemoan her sorrows. She had three divorces behind her, two failed self-employment ventures, and a variety of ailments, including a recurring rash below the right knee. She complained and complained. The Dalai Lama let her words flow for a while, then took a deep breath and responded. "Mimimimi, next," he said, without turning his head. It was by far the best thing I've heard in years. His Holiness apparently had no desire to listen to the whining and lamenting of a person in one of the richest countries in the world. With cruel wars in so many regions, people starving, and a dirty sea filled with plastic rubbish, had this woman—who'd only been granted a few seconds with one of the wisest men in the world—really talked about her *rash*?

I have zero understanding of why people behave like this, and I stood up, loudly applauding his response. But I was pretty much alone: most of the room felt sorry for her. "While you complain, others are saving the world," I thought. At the same time, my heart told me she probably couldn't do anything about her limited view of the world. In her reality, she had simply spoken of what was weighing her down.

In nature, everything is in harmony. Animals don't need qi gong or sound therapy to restore their balance. They simply throw themselves into the mix, communicating with all other organisms, and following nature's great plan. Imagine if they complained. Imagine if they went to the doctor for stress and exhaustion. The hare in the meadow does not perform the Five Tibetans before he sets off running; he simply has no time. The bird doesn't sit on the branch and say, "I don't want to fly. I don't feel like it today." If you find yourself repeatedly relying on external stimuli, you've probably stopped listening to your inner self. Gratitude and humility could be your route to greater happiness and success.

On that note, there's a good practice I can highly recommend. In the following section, I've written down a few of the things for which I am grateful, and on the right-hand side, I'd ask you to note down everything for which *you* are grateful. Whenever I'm not feeling good, I read my gratitude list. By the time I reach the tenth word, I usually find tears of gratitude rolling down my face.

Weather • ______________________

Health • ______________________

Family • ______________________

Neighbors • ______________________

Money • ______________________

Other people • ______________________

Railway • ______________________

Food • ______________________

Service • ______________________

Public servants • ______________________

Internet • ______________________

Technology • ______________________

If you're having trouble thinking of things, here are a few pointers to get you thinking:

- Friends
- Seeing
- Hearing
- Tasting
- Smelling
- Dancing
- Teeth
- Flowers
- Toothbrushes, etc.

My Journey to Within

During my time in Brazil, I got to experience a lot of amazing things. If the world has a central point of energy, for me, it's definitely South America. There's one particular story from there that only my closest confidants know.

I was living with a friend's family in a mountain village in the south of the country, a place so remote that the bus arrived only every four days. One night, we heard a knock at the door. I started and waited for my hosts to answer. Since I didn't speak much Portuguese at that time, the deep male voice was all I could make out. It called my name—more than once. Inwardly, I told myself that there must be some mistake: I didn't know anyone there, and nobody knew me. Apparently, I was wrong.

At the kitchen table sat a man clothed in fur and, in his hair, twigs were woven together to form a sort of crown. This impressive individual was an indigenous inhabitant, the shaman of the region. He took me in his arms and began to speak. Completely amazed, I listened to the translation of my equally surprised friend.

The shaman was glad that I was finally there, he said, because he had been waiting for a long time. He confirmed that I was Tobi from Germany. When I nodded, he turned to me directly. "You're probably very shocked, but don't be afraid," he said. "I've simply come to tell you that all will be well. Your first years of life have been tough. You've been antagonized, you cannot deal with hierarchies, and you don't know which profession to pursue. You think you can't do anything. Do you remember the pediatrician who told your mother not to worry if you were not able to function in the conventional system?" Open-mouthed, I shook my head. "My job," he continued, "is to tell you that someday, you will speak in front of thousands of people, and it will come very easily to you. You'll write books, bring joy to people, and allow them to grow, as I do here on a small scale. We are brothers."

I was completely taken aback by the situation, but *did* recall a dim memory of my desperate mother taking me to the doctor. She was worried about me, and had wanted to check whether everything was okay. The doctor calmed her nerves and said that, one day, I would speak in front of a large audience. I used to believe that life was just a coincidence, but is this really true? When you think about your life so far, have there been situations where, even though others were trying to encourage you on your path, you were not ready to see it?

If you've read this far, I'd like to share with you my spiritual teachers—since hopefully, by now, you recognize that spirituality is as much a part of the wheel of life as all other areas. Laura Seiler, whose book and podcast I've often relied upon, has supported me many times on my spiritual journey. Bahar Yilmaz and Jeffrey Kastenmüller, whose seminars I've had the privilege of attending, have a special way of not taking things too seriously, of addressing spirituality in a fresh, modern manner. Finally, there's Ellen Michels, who has a fantastic gift for high vibration. To round off the chapter, I want to share a thought I believe in: that the inside reflects the outside, and the outside the inner life. Start "tidying up" the inside, and you'll see a lot of external changes, too.

Past and Present

The past is one of the main reasons why people fail to succeed. I hear this countless times in my seminars. Some people, for example, have very violent stories from their childhoods. The good news is that there are some great exercises for making peace with what has gone by. Much more important, however, is your attitude toward what has happened to you in life.

One of my favorite ways of thinking about the past was learned from my Japanese host family in Tokyo, whom I stayed with more than twenty years ago when attempting to learn Japanese. I lived in a traditional family home. My host father (Oto-san) cultivated bonsai trees and worked for hours with these remarkably maintenance-intensive plants. My host mother (Oka-san) was a tea ceremony mistress, and taught me about patience and age-old customs. I was particularly impressed by the precious tea bowls made of thin porcelain, all of them hand-painted. If such a bowl breaks, it is not thrown away, but fused together again using gold. This creates a new treasure with beautiful lines, and means that every bowl is unique. By doing this, the Japanese highlight the beauty of broken things. They believe that, once broken, a thing becomes even more valuable. They believe that if something has suffered damage and has a story, it is all the more beautiful as a result.

The same applies to humans. The things you've gone through do not make your life "uglier" or "worse," as much as it may seem like that to you. It's up to us to make our scars and tears golden again. To go further with the metaphor: you have not been broken for good, but repaired with gold and actually made better. The gold represents your friends and family, who are there for you even in the darkest of times. The shards are your painful past experiences, and the bowl is your life.

You can get back on your feet, learn from the past, and become a better person as a result of all your effort and pain. Better yet, you can become an illuminated path, a lighthouse for others, so they do not have to go through the same. Your experience is not in vain. You can wear your scars with pride and as a badge of honor. You can say, "Look at what I've been through. It's made me who I am today, and I can face any challenge."

Nobody has ever had a perfect life, and nobody will ever have. It is up to us whether we suffer or choose to share our knowledge with others. There is no need to be ashamed of what has happened to you; everything has a reason. This is something I strongly believe in. If, for example, I had not spent so many years in a sect that forbade me to communicate with the outside world, my current sense of mission would not be so great. I say this despite my suffering and the fact that my will was broken.

The more we resist, the more we complain and object to what has happened to us, the more likely our path is to remain in the dark, for all our experiences are deeply rooted within us. In contrast, the moment when we accept these things and find use and purpose in our struggle and pain can be very healing.

In doing this, we transform something that may be ugly to us into something beautiful and inspiring to others. If what we have lived through can serve as an inspiration to those around us, this makes the pain and suffering worth it. Each chapter of our book requires a new version of ourselves. Until we've accepted the importance of being broken, we won't be able to turn the page.

Write down what parts of your life could be useful to others when mended with gold:

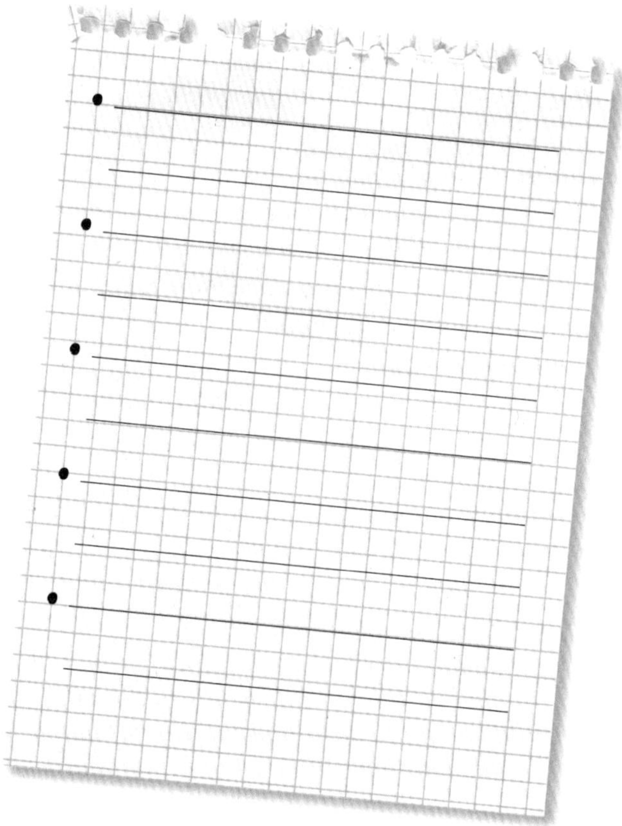

Stay True to Your Path

"Always check the side effects!" You'll no doubt recognize this sentence from medication ads—and this last chapter is something similar. In it, I want to offer you one final piece of advice, which is: stick to your path! If you implement the tips from this book on a consistent basis, you'll be able to effect a lot of change. Starting today, the sentence you'll hear most often is, "You have changed completely." And understand this well: for energy vampires, change is a problem, if not a complete disaster. Energy vampires want things to stay as they are.

Successful people see the future and change as a chance to grow. When birthdays roll around, one often hears wishes such as, "Never change!" Beware: these are the wishes of energy vampires! Of course, it's only natural that people don't want things to change. But we were not born to pay our bills and die. If you continue to make yourself small, hide yourself, and be scared of any and everything, it won't help anyone, least of all you. Live your dream, my friend—and not the dreams of others, who enrich themselves at the expense of your energy and vigor.

Make no mistake, the way will be very, very tenuous. There is only one question that can trigger change in your life, and that is: are you ready to pay the price? Are you ready to put your ego behind you, allow yourself to be polished and, in a couple of years, lead a life that others could only dream of? You were born to enjoy life in all its facets. Let yourself be shaped by its edges and sharp corners in order to shine in your full glory. Learn to understand the statement "You've changed completely" as a compliment. When two people clash, the one who triumphs is the one with greater energy. Draw energy from this message. Celebrate your rough edges. Diamonds are not round! Trust in life and in the fact that whatever happens to you is intended to polish and refine you. Remember: the most beautiful diamonds are the ones that are cut most elaborately. Do not let anyone dissuade you from your path. Trust in yourself, your inner strength, and that strength that you draw from every life lesson.

The best thing you can do for yourself and your development is to stay focused, keep your goals in mind, and gather people around you who share the same outlook. People fail because they do not stick to their path. They fill their lives with distractions such as television, social media, or computer games. They numb themselves so as not to feel the pain. Do not join them! Your passion is what should occupy your time. Spend your time visualizing it. Have you ever been gripped by a singular desire from morning to evening, one that was constantly in your mind, that you couldn't get rid of? That's what happens when you're on the right path. You're in the flow. It's the feeling of being in love. You wake up without an alarm clock and tackle each day full of joy. Each and every second, you pursue the thing that sets your world alight; you alone decide which way to go. Grow at every step, and burn! Shepherd others onto the right path and bring them along with you. This is the path you embarked on by opening this book—a path that all happy and successful people have also embarked on and pursue each day. You are currently walking in their footsteps, and I wish you a great deal of enjoyment in seeing where you get to.

About the Author

A former flight attendant with a learning disability, and now a university lecturer, Tobias Beck has become one of Europe's most-loved speakers and hosts life-changing seminars and personal consultations. He explains, in a humorous fashion, how the principles of success and motivational psychology can work for others too. His Bewohnerfrei® ("Liberated") podcast hit # 1 on the iTunes download charts upon its release and reaches an audience of millions online.

www.tobias-beck.com